# To Catch a Sparrow

## Eva Holt

This novel is entirely a work of fiction. The names, characters and incidents portrayed in it are the work of the author's imagination. Any resemblance to actual persons, living or dead, events or localities is entirely coincidental.

Proofread by Laë Proofreads

Paperback formatting by Laë Proofreads

To the ones with your finger on the trigger,
don't pull it.

*To Victoria,*
*You told me my words saved you that day. But the truth is, yours*
*saved mine. We wouldn't be reading this book had your words not*
*been permanently engraved on my heart. Thank you for staying.*
*Please always stay.*
*EHW*

# Trigger Warnings

18+ read

This story contains potentially disturbing or offensive content that may be harmful to some readers. Examples of this include:

- Extreme violence and death

- Suicide

- Blood and gore

- Illness

- Grief / loss

- Survivors guilt

- Graphic language

- Mental health

- Use of weapons

- Explicit sex scenes

- Use of drugs

- Unconventional HEA

This is not a fairy tale. This is a written version of the darkest parts of my mind and I encourage you to read responsibly. This story romanticizes uncomfortable themes such as suicide, murder, and drug use.

*If you intend to turn the page, I hope you enjoy the Ryde.*

# Playlist

My Curse — Killswitch Engage

Hush Now — VOILA

Luminary — Joel Sunny

Smells Like Teen Spirit — Stevie Howie

When I'm Like This — Kathleen Regan

Wicked Game — Lusaint

Living and Existing — CJ Starnes

Bitter End — Gold Souls

Bad Habits — Nerv

Please Don't Go — Stephanie Rainey

In the Air Tonight — Stephanie Rainey

The Other Side — Ruelle

The Silence — Morgan Clae

Last November — MGK

Skin and Bones — David Kushner

The Night We Met — Lord Huron

\*\*\*

# Chapter 1

*Devina*

*Y*ou came for me.

My feet hit the pavement, and with each impact, I'm thrust forward. I try to stomp away her last words with every step. The wind is my enemy today, pushing against me. I usually run through the streets of Boston on sunny fall mornings. The cool air chills me just enough to warrant the long sleeves that I can't live without.

"My Curse" by Killswitch Engage is on full blast in my headphones. My music is loud, but not loud enough to drown out the echo of her last words.

It's been two weeks since I learned the life-altering, earth-shattering news, but to tell you the truth, it's been months since my body has been withering away.

Six years ago, I survived a masked gunman and a fire on the same night. Turns out, I didn't just get lucky. Death was coming for me, and this time, she was angry.

Meningiomas.

*Cancer.*

Brain cancer.

The kind that kills you with no miracle elixir. Not that I would have taken one if one existed. I wouldn't want to endure the pain that comes with that. A lot of people do. Those people have something to live for.

So here I am—running...from my pain, from the past, from reality. However, each run is becoming shorter and more challenging. Some people are lucky with non-threatening tumors that decorate their spinal cord. Mine comes with a healthy menu of symptoms and an immaculately placed ring of tumors that will eventually lead to my death.

My mind was already a dark, dangerous place. Maybe the cancer was born from my thoughts, taking up residence on my spinal cord and traveling north, physical nuggets of the hatred and self-loathing I have held close for all of these years.

I used to spend hours running for the adrenaline. Now, running is just a constant reminder of how frail I've become. I usually start strong, but my bones tire and muscles ache quickly. I'm one sharp impact away from injury, but I can't stop. Not until I find the man who killed my sister. And I certainly can't kill anyone if I can't keep myself in shape.

As I round the block and head back to the estate, I'm greeted by my brother's guards who buzz me through the gate.

I make my way past my brother's new black car in the driveway and up the stairs. I didn't hear Declan behind me until it was too late, and I nearly backed into him.

"Are you going to be ready for dinner tonight?" There are no pleasantries—not that I expected any from him. My brother is aggressive, abrasive, and only cares about one thing: money. It would be easy to be angry with him, but he lost Scarlet just like I did. I can't tell how genuine his concern and generosity are, but on the rare occasions that I do speak up, he reminds me that all his decisions are centered around keeping his only remaining sister alive.

Declan threw himself into saving our family business after my father and sister burned. I'm like a gnat to him; aimlessly floating around, always there when he would rather move on alone. I'm an inconvenience, and he frequently reminds me. Maybe he does love me. But our pain is too large, devouring the new world we were forced into. He's been my guardian until I turned eighteen, but continued to care for me after. Maybe he hates me as much as I hate myself for being the one who made it out.

"Yes, I'm just heading up to get ready." I let the corners of my lips curl, trying to convince us both that I'm happy to still be here, among the living, and turn to leave.

Tonight is the family's monthly dinner. The family consists of the important members of Declan's company, and by company, I mean an enterprise that is criminal in nature. Don't get me wrong, there are plenty of legitimate businesses that help him build our wealth, but I'm not completely naive to believe our name isn't rooted in something more sinister.

My participation is in person only. I'm not to speak unless spoken to, and I'm almost certain that I'm only there to be ogled and keep the gents from becoming too drunk and unruly. They may be utter brutes, but they would remain gentlemen in front of Declan Sullivan's baby sister.

Stepping out of the shower, I gaze at myself in the mirror. My scars have faded to pink and white. Subtle against my pale skin, but still very apparent. When I stare at them long enough, I can still feel the fire melting my skin away. The heat I endured was one I almost welcomed some days, when the memory of everything that was taken from me becomes too much to bear.

Tonight, I'll wear my emerald dress with long sleeves to cover the burn marks that crept up my left arm. The color matches my eyes and enhances the copper in my hair, distracting others from everything I want to keep hidden. I shouldn't care what I look like. I should wear my scars like a badge of honor—I survived. But the simple realization that I survived is always quickly followed by the reminder that *she didn't*.

I hate how I look beneath my sleeves, but I hate myself more—the person I am beneath the scars is broken and jagged. Anyone who dares get too close will get cut. I should have died with Scarlet. Most days, the only thought that keeps me going is the sheer determination to kill a man. The invisible man. The man who took it all from me as if it were just another Tuesday. When I imagine his eyes turning lifeless beneath me, the warmth I feel in my scars transfers to my hands as I imagine his blood running over my fingers until it turns cold.

It's almost cruel that the day I learned of my condition, I learned about my newest suspect. I don't have his real name yet, but my best friend, Taylor, narrowed it down to someone in the Italian family. I should have known. To say there is bad blood between the Irish and Italian families would be an understatement.

After the fire, there was a brief time when Declan seemed to find happiness in a woman, but her abrupt departure sealed his heart away for good. She came from an Italian family that rivals ours. While he would never share specifics with me, I know she's the reason no one was to associate with them. I'm caged and sheltered from a lot of truth, but I'm certain the Italians had something to do with my brother's downward spiral, and for that, I hate them even more.

I was given no real expiration date, but the doctor assured me I have another year before my body shuts down and my brain becomes a pile of mush.

*One year.*

That seems like adequate time to get your affairs in order, but when one of your life goals is tracking down and killing an invisible man, it now feels like the ultimate challenge—and I hate to lose. I certainly can't lose before the last grain of sand falls through the hourglass.

With my hair in place and my dress zipped tight, I step into my most comfortable heels and make my way to the dining room.

Declan's men have started to flow in after leaving their weapons in the foyer. The twelve-person dining table is full of mostly familiar faces, minus the two seats to my right.

"We have two guests joining us momentarily," Declan states to the group as if he's been reading my mind. "The Totaro family is sending two representatives."

The crowd snickers. I know I've heard this name before, but I can't seem to pinpoint where.

"Behave," he commands, as he adjusts the cuff links of his crisp blue button down. "There are only a few terms that need to be negotiated, but once this is complete, we'll have a sturdier grasp on the individuals who thought it was a good idea to slither into our territory and more men to help us take care of it."

A knock at the door turns everyone's eyes, and I brace myself. We never have guests at our home. This is a rule. Taylor wasn't even allowed to visit after the fire, and I've been friends with him for years.

Two men in suits make their way to Declan and shake his hand at the end of the table before spotting their seats next to me.

*Italians.*

My blood runs cold. I wonder if I could be sitting next to the man who pulled the trigger seven years ago.

"Thank you for the warm welcome. Luca and I are just as excited as you are to see this arrangement come to fruition," the older man says as they sit.

Luca, the younger one, nods in agreement and places his napkin in his lap.

The servers pour wine, and the men begin chatting about business. A business that I'm not so privy to and not the least bit interested in.

I've learned that the older man's name is Ronnie, and he certainly isn't the man I want to kill. I can tell by his voice. By his scent. Luca is too young and shorter than the suspect; I couldn't possibly forget. The realization helps my shoulders ease slightly. My fingers twist in my lap as I try to put thoughts of that night out of my mind until—

"Well, there is only one last item on the agenda," Luca states, satisfied with whatever they had just come to terms with. "Who is the lucky bride?"

I arch a brow toward Declan, inwardly kicking myself for not paying attention for the past hour.

"We have a few women who would be willing and eager to help this alliance happen," he says as he waves the server over, requesting a stack of papers.

Bride? Is he marrying someone off for an alliance?

"Bridget is nearly twenty-five. She's a registered nurse and plays piano. Patricia is twenty-seven. She's a bit of a wildflower but could use some taming if you know what I mean." The men chuckle at Declan's description of my cousins.

I begin to roll my eyes, but am struck in the head with a deliciously devious idea. If I can get into the Italian family, it'll increase my chances of finding the fucker who killed my sister. This might be the best shot I have, and with my time slipping away so quickly, I'd be a fool not to take it. My mind is working overtime, but it hasn't quite made the connection with my mouth, and my mouth is already moving.

"I'll do it." I can't swallow the words back.

A piece of silverware clinks as it falls to a plate, and everyone at the table stops talking. All eyes are on me. Declan has his glass halfway to his mouth when his brows arch in surprise as he stiffens in his chair. The air around us seems to have thickened enough to hide the steam that I'm sure is coming out of my brother's ears.

I adjust in my seat and give the men my sweetest smile. "I will marry into the Totaro family," I say politely. "If they'll have me." I give the Italians a little head tilt and bat my lashes. They don't seem disappointed.

"Well, it's nice to see someone so eager to unite our families, Mr. Sullivan." Luca raises his glass toward Declan.

Mumbles between the men around me grow louder as I instantly regret my decision. My heart slams against the walls of my chest. My breath becomes quick under the scrutiny of my older brother.

Declan's face turns as red as his hair, but I know he won't challenge me in front of everyone. There will be consequences for my talking out of turn, but in my mind, there is no other way.

"Certainly," he says, but I can feel him seething beneath the surface.

The men raise their glasses to share a celebratory clink, and I nearly melt into my seat. My nerves are getting the best of me, but I can hardly contain my excitement. They have no idea what they just agreed to, but I guess I don't either.

The rest of the bourbon is sipped over a light conversation while I'm left to stew in my latest poor choice. Well, I guess the quality of my choice is yet to be determined. Still, I'm left a little unsettled and slightly overwhelmed.

When the men stand to leave, I receive kind departing words from everyone before Declan corners me in the foyer. His fists are clenched at his sides as he looks down at me with fury.

"What the hell were you thinking, Devina?" he says through clenched teeth.

"You know that Bridget and Patricia were horrible offers. Bridget doesn't want to be married...to a man, and Patricia would be a complete embarrassment," I reason flippantly.

"Were you even listening to the conversation? Do you know who you are marrying?" He leans back on his heels, crossing his arms over his chest.

"No, but does it matter? You've taken care of me long enough," I bite back.

This seems to resonate with him, and I can see the wheels turning. He may not be happy, but he will comply. He has no choice now.

"We are getting paid a pretty penny for the Irish bride. If I knew it would be you, I would have increased the price." I wonder if he meant for that to be said out loud, but that's Declan; always looking at the bottom line. "Fine, I'll allow it," he concludes as if he could change the outcome now.

"Great." Hesitant to show too much excitement with my twisted new plan, I nod in agreement, smile, and reach up to scratch the stubble he's allowed to take up residence on his sharp jaw. He acts like he hates it, but it reminds him of when we were younger and I'd tease him for being such a grumpy old man. He halfheartedly hides a grin, and I know I'm not truly in trouble.

I turn to make my way upstairs and let tonight's events sink in.

How could I possibly fall asleep with an entire kill plan that needs to be perfected? After tossing and turning for nearly an hour, I jumped online for a quick internet search.

There are four eligible brothers. I wonder which one it will be. Luca and Philippe are good candidates, although Luca didn't let on that he was the intended groom this evening. Ryder? Logan? My brother did a great job of keeping our business off the radar, unlike the Totaro family. They are notorious for being ruthless...and stunning. All four of them. Their sketchy behavior may be newsworthy, but you could just as easily find tabloids sharing their latest dining experiences and extracurricular outings with women. For a family rumored to be dark and twisted, they sure enjoyed the spotlight.

Based on looks alone, I should consider myself lucky to have any of them. I'm pretty enough, but they appear flawless and poised—even in candid shots.

I switch my phone off, having decided that Philippe is the likeliest groom to be. He is only three years older. Ryder is nearly a decade older, and Logan, the oldest, now lives abroad. Closing my eyes and feeling slightly at ease now, I close my eyes and let sleep take me.

# Chapter 2

*Ryder*

It's half past ten when Ronnie walks into my office like he won the damn lottery.

"All done, boss," he quips proudly with the clap of his meaty hands.

"What is the final number?" I ask, not looking up from my laptop.

"Four million."

That causes me to pause mid-stroke.

"That's less than what we anticipated. What changed?" It's common knowledge that Declan Sullivan is as greedy as they come. I sent the guys out with a budget of six million.

"You always underestimate me," he complains. "I started at three. Anyway, they're going to facilitate the mergers we presented, and I think you'll be happy with the *other arrangement*." He cocks a brow my way. "The girl practically jumped at the chance to marry into the family. Her brother wasn't too happy about it, but—"

"What do you mean 'her brother'?" I stand, my curiosity piqued. We were presented with a couple of options before the meeting. None of the candidates have siblings that I can recall, and none were supposed to be at the dinner. If they were, I would have made it a point to go myself.

"Devina Sullivan." He purrs her name as if it were sugar dripping off his tongue.

This is a surprise. I haven't even considered her an option. Declan keeps her under lock and key. Intrigued, I shoot an email to my younger brother, Philippe, to do some research. He's our resident computer nerd.

From our prior research, both women are fairly attractive but, Declan's cousin, Bridget, seems like the best candidate. The other just looks like trouble.

"Well, that's interesting. I wonder what's wrong with her. I'm not sure if someone could pay me enough to marry off one of my siblings." I raise a brow.

"That's the odd thing, boss. She volunteered. I could tell Declan was just as surprised as we were when she did. She's in a completely different league than the other two. Nothing is wrong with her. Actually, something was intriguing about her. I can't quite put my finger on it." He walks over to the bar cart to pour himself a celebratory drink.

The bottom line is that it doesn't matter who marries into the family. My father is looking to step away from the business and leave it to one of his children, but only if we are married. Something about commitment to the family and a display of maturity. As if we haven't been groomed our entire lives to be cunning and savage.

The four of us have already discussed how operations would work, running it as a team. Something my father doesn't want to hear about. So, for now, we've agreed that one of us will suck it up and get married. In the end, we will change things as we see fit, but we need the old man to step down first.

I'm partially relieved that the transaction went smoothly, but there is a part of me that feels unsettled. It's no secret that our families have had their share of differences over the decades. So, why was Declan so eager to cast his baby sister away? Maybe she can't have children. In our situation, it's a non-issue. We don't need her to produce a child. We aren't in the fucking Middle Ages and we don't view women as cattle. I also have two younger brothers who will eventually get married and have children of their own.

Perhaps there isn't anything wrong with her, but there has to be a reason she was so willing to volunteer.

*What are you hiding, Devina Sullivan?*
"Thanks, Ronnie." I raise my glass and nod, dismissing him.

Taking my thoughts to the balcony, I light a smoke and try to figure out our next move. I agreed to marry one of the women from the Sullivan clan. Not that I wanted to. Dealing with Declan is the last thing that I want after what transpired with Michaela, an unfortunate loss I've spent years trying to forget. Now he's here, asking for help when he should be begging for forgiveness. Coward.

The ping of my phone interrupts my thoughts and a photo of Devina Sullivan flashes on the screen with a note from Philippe.

**Philippe: Nice.**

Tossing my cigarette in the ashtray and heading back to my desk, I pull up the rest of the file he prepared.

Yes, she is *nice*. She's fucking gorgeous. Scanning through the file, I learn that she's twenty-four. She's probably a better fit for Philippe based on age. It appears she works at one of her brother's offices. A newspaper clipping shows an article from several years ago. A house fire—no known cause, but a few family members perished. *Interesting.* What's more interesting is the amount of ownership she'll inherit once she's married. I wonder if she's aware.

I glance at the only photo occupying my desk. Torn on the edges and creased, it's forever preserved in a silver frame. My sweet Michaela and I. We were so young in this photo. It was taken about ten years ago. Our friendship bloomed easily and it showed. The photo encompassed our innocence before I knew we were to be wed. Before she was taken from me.

Declan is the reason we are even searching for a bride. He's the reason our territory is being invaded by the Bratva. Declan *fucking* Sullivan is the reason I now have only the memory of the woman I was supposed to marry.

There has to be something I'm missing. Would he be dumb enough to plant his sister in our home to gather information? Well, I'm sure he is, but I'm not sure what he's looking for. Like the serpent whispering promises in the garden, a thought enters my mind, and it's too delicious to ignore. Mr. Sullivan took everything from me that night, and after years of waiting for the right time to strike, a stunning opportunity has presented itself. *An eye for an eye, Mr. Sullivan.*

Originally, I needed this deal to gain shares in the Sullivan Corporation. But if I can get Devina to sign over her shares, we'd have the majority vote. By the time I'm done with her, she'll be more than willing to sign them over. Women are easy, flippant creatures swayed by romance and a good fuck. I should have her eating out of the palm of my hand in no time. It will be the biggest *fuck you* to Declan before they both take a bullet to the head.

I glance back at my screen; at the image of Devina, dialing Philippe. She looks so innocent and unknowing. Her eyes are what captivate me. Guarded with a hint of fragility. Pure.

"Who is Devina?" he asks instead of greeting me.

"Declan Sullivan's sister," I answer.

He sighs, clearly irritated with me. "Obviously. Why am I looking her up?"

"She's the bride."

There's a beat of silence before he responds. "Are you okay? What do you need me to do?"

The ideas run through my mind until I land on my newest desire.

"I want to break her." I fill him in on the plan to take over Sullivan Corporations.

"You know she has nothing to do with this. She was just a kid,

Ryde."

"He'll pay." I pinch my brows together and close my eyes, trying to overcome my conscience, which isn't accepting my desire to ruin an innocent woman. "She's the price, and he will pay. I need to know everything there is to know. Not just her birthday and her fucking job title. No detail is too small. I want to know her fucking favorite flower. Get me something I can use."

"I'll see what I can do." He isn't happy, but he'll do it.

My mind is made up. I've resolved to jump into this marriage with a lot more enthusiasm than originally anticipated.

What is the saying? Killing two birds with one stone?

And what a beautiful little sparrow she is.

# Chapter 3

## *Devina*

T aylor sighs over the phone. "You agreed to *what?*"

I can imagine him pinching the bridge of his nose in frustration.

"I agreed to get us closer to the man who took everything from me—from *us*. I just narrowed down our search. I am taking one for the team here." I spent the past twenty minutes giving my best friend a rundown of last night's events.

While the initial reports showed that Scarlet and my father were the only remains found, it was later discovered that Taylor's mother was found in the back of the house. No gunshot wounds. She wasn't supposed to be there, just an unfortunate casualty in the war that ensued that night. The unfortunate casualty is the spark that ignited Taylor's hatred for the underworld altogether. Before that, we were just kids waiting to take on everything the world had to offer. After? After, we were bitter and bruised, but determined to find answers.

"Vi, I love you. You know I'm in this with you, but do you hear yourself? You are willingly entering the lion's den." His aggravation bubbles beneath the surface.

"I'm running out of time," I reason in my best annoying little sister voice. Taylor is the only one who knows about my diagnosis. The silence on the other end is telling me that he knows I'm right.

"This will change a lot of our plans. For one, it will make our communication more difficult. You think your new husband will approve of you hanging out with another guy?"

"You aren't just another guy. You're my best friend. You're practically my brother," I say.

"Your best friend and co-conspirator." He chuckles.

"He won't need to know that. Besides, you're family. Where I go, you go, right?"

"Sure, well, we have our work cut out for us. How do you see all of this going down?"

Taylor is as loyal as they come. He may not like the unexpected change of plans, but he will be my ride or die until the very end.

"I want him to burn."

A daydream that occupies my mind more than I am willing to admit. I run my fingers over the scars on my left arm and relish in the feeling of satisfaction I'll feel watching his skin melt away from his body. His screams will slowly evaporate as death consumes him. How proud Scarlet will be.

"You still there?" Taylor brings me back to reality.

"Still here." I clear my throat. "Hey, I have to get going. Declan sent me a note that I have my first dress fitting today, and our pending nuptials will be happening as soon as possible."

"You get a real wedding?" he jokes. "Usually, these deals happen in a courthouse on the sly. It's not like you love each other. Do you even know which one you are marrying? It will be easier to research if I know."

"No, but I have a feeling it's Philippe. I'd start there," I say. "And as much as I love you, you know you can't be there, right? I want to keep you a secret as long as I can."

"You know I'll have eyes in the sky before the big day. Love you, sis." I don't think he realizes how much I wish he were my brother. Taylor is two years older, but his mother started working for us when we were in elementary school. Most of my childhood memories are sprinkled with his laughter and the consequences that came from his bad ideas.

After we hang up, I pull on some leggings and a long-sleeved T-shirt. Day-two hair will have to suffice.

When I hit the bottom of the stairs, I can hear shuffling in the kitchen. Darlene is attempting to make a cappuccino.

"Hey there!" I smile. "Need some help?" Darlene is the house manager Declan hired a week ago. I hope she sticks around. It makes me uneasy to imagine Declan in this house all alone. We haven't maintained a full staff since my father ruled this house, but Darlene seems promising. She's a quiet woman, a few years older than me. She is radiant, resembling someone who should be on the cover of a magazine instead of running Declan's errands.

"You're a lifesaver, Miss Sullivan. I can't get this thing to agree with me!"

"Darlene, I've told you a million times. Please call me Vi, everyone does. And I'm not your boss. Your boss is the guy with a stick up his—"

"Up his..." Declan enters the room, adjusting his tie.

"Oh great, you're here! Are you taking me to get a dress today?" I change the subject while Darlene averts her eyes and scurries away.

"I'd love to, Devina, but your little stunt last night has me running around in circles today trying to finalize some things that have to be done before your wedding."

"When exactly is my wedding?" I guess as the bride, I should know.

"Tuesday. Be at church at four." He presses a few buttons and waits while his coffee brews into the to-go mug I got him last Christmas. He must be fond of Darlene. He's had to teach her how to use the cappuccino machine three times. Any of his men would have been taken out to pasture by now.

How can he be so casual about this? Sure, it was my idea, but it would be nice if I had gotten something more than an Outlook calendar invite and a waiting car. Is he even planning on taking me? Is this going to be a photographed affair, or a simple family-only situation? None of it should matter, but a tiny piece of my heart longs to enjoy a sliver of the experience. It will be the only wedding I'll ever have, after all.

He straightens his tie and squares his shoulders, turning to leave. His usual stoic demeanor falters slightly as he pauses in the doorway. "I know why you're doing this, Devina."

Instant dread pours into my chest, making it difficult to breathe. He could put an end to this before it even starts. But would he? Would he truly stand in the way of seeking the revenge I've worked so hard to achieve? It's so close, I only need to reach and it would brush against my fingertips.

Without turning to look at me, he lowers his head. "I won't stop you, but I don't agree with it. Nothing will bring her back."

My stomach sinks, but the relief of his words makes my heart soar. Scarlet is not a topic we discuss openly. She's the ghost that wanders these halls and provides a slight buffer between us. We grieve her in our own, secluded way. Alone. Always alone. I can't be surprised that once he had time to calm down last night, he was able to see my real intentions.

On the third anniversary of the fire, Declan and I got drunk, and I confessed the details of what happened that night. I wanted them to pay in blood. Declan didn't think I could be capable of such things. I was the baby; he was ten years my senior. I was innocent in his eyes. But I saw a glimmer of recognition in his eyes that night. Like he was meeting a new, dark version of me for the first time. A version that was not so unlike him.

We never spoke of it again. And since we rarely talk about Scarlet, our parents, or the unfortunate events that left us orphans, the memories float around, haunting us every day, unwilling to let us move forward.

I swallow down the last of my coffee and the feeling of longing, knowing today is nothing like what I would have imagined. Scarlet should be here with me, but the urge to stab the fucker that took her from me gives me the will to put one foot in front of the other and take the next step toward sealing his fate.

There aren't many options for what I'm looking for in this dress shop. I was greeted by Ms. Penny, a petite, round woman with bottlecap glasses. She's cheery and eager to help me *say yes to the dress*. Unfortunately, most of these dresses are strapless, and the ones with sleeves look dated and are likely for women far beyond my age.

"Are you ready to show me?" Ms. Penny calls from the other side of the door.

The dress is mostly lace. Gold embellishments are sprinkled subtly throughout the bodice, which hugs me in all the right places. The gown is a modest princess, flowing down to the floor. The only problem—the sweetheart neckline leaves most of my chest and arms bare.

"Ready as I'll ever be." I take one final look before turning to face the wall of mirrors.

Hurrying past Ms. Penny, I situate myself on the faux stage.

The door rings as someone enters, and Ms. Penny excuses herself to assist the customer.

Returning moments later, she makes her way around me to fluff my dress. Catching a glimpse of the damage to my arm, she pauses and attempts to regain her composure.

"It's okay," I say, knowing she's wondering how a young lady such as myself could have earned herself such a gruesome scar. "It doesn't hurt," I assure her, knowing that is usually the first question people have.

"I'm sorry, dear, I don't mean to stare." She busies herself fluffing the rest of my skirt and pinching the back of my bodice.

I gaze at myself and believe it or not, I feel beautiful. I look like a real bride. I mean, I am a real bride. If this dress had sleeves, I would buy it in a heartbeat. But I can't bring myself to commit to it. I imagine everyone present would look at me the way Ms. Penny just did.

This may be an arrangement, but I would hate for people to think it's arranged because Declan Sullivan's baby sister is too deformed and disgusting to get herself a husband on her own.

"Can I have just a minute?" I ask.

"Sure thing, I'll go check on my other guest and be right back." She smiles and looks grateful for an escape.

I pull the hair tie from my hair, allowing my locks to fall around my shoulders. Gathering half of it up with my hand to see if I could distract from my insecurities, I huff at the realization that this is just not going to be the dress for me.

Mrs. Penny returns, "Sorry about that, dear. How do we feel about this one?"

"I don't think this one is going to work." I tell her, "I need one of those with sleeves. For obvious reasons." I point to the chair that holds the three long-sleeved dresses I selected earlier. "I'd like to change now." I step down from the stage and make my way back to the changing room before anyone can witness the tears that have welled in the corner of my eyes.

When I emerge, Mrs. Penny is waiting with a smile, and the three dresses I can't help but hate in comparison to the one I just stepped out of, hang on the rack next to the register.

"Which one are we saying yes to, dear?" She smiles kindly.

"Surprise me," I say, leaving her shocked. Right now, we are both disappointed. "Look, I really love the last one, but if I'm not wearing that, I don't have a preference. You have a beautiful store, full of extravagant dresses. Any one of these will do."

She beams at the compliment. "You will be a beautiful bride, miss. I'll make some small adjustments for your measurements and send it to the address you provided."

I thank her and leave to head home. The entire experience took more of an emotional toll than I thought it would, and I could use a run.

# Chapter 4

*Ryder*

⑾|⑾|⑾ Hush Now — VOILA ⑾|⑾|⑾

Stepping into the dress shop is a risk, but it's a risk I'm willing to take. Superstitions don't exist when the marriage is arranged, right? The image of Devina Sullivan had invaded my mind for most of the night. I wasn't planning on meeting her face to face, but I do have the overwhelming need to see her in person.

First thing this morning, I set this appointment and sent Declan a message to have her here. He didn't respond, but I'm glad he followed my instructions.

I'm greeted by the shop owner and I inform her that I would be waiting for my fiancé to select a dress.

"I promise I won't look," I assure her. "I just can't stay away from her. Please keep this between us." I give her my best smile and a wink.

She gives me a conspiratorial look and gestures for me to have a seat in the unoccupied lobby behind the fitting area.

"It's okay, it doesn't hurt." A velvety voice carries through the small shop. My thoughts pause. My pulse races. *Devina.*

I consider peering around the wall to see her, but something stops me. Moments later, Penny comes back to check on me.

"Everything's going well?" I quietly ask my co-conspirator.

"The poor dear. I don't mean to pry, but she seems a little self-conscious about displaying her arms." I tilt my head, wondering what she is referring to. "But not to worry, sir, she will find the perfect dress."

"Thank you, please let me know when she's done and I'll

settle the tab," I say, taking a seat in one of the plush chairs.

She nearly swoons. "Lucky girl!" She scurries back to the viewing room.

Watching her leave, I can't help myself. As I peek around the corner, I catch her as she drops the hair she was holding. Soft, copper, and gold tresses cascade around her shoulders. From this angle, I can see her face, but I'm sure she can't see me. She stares forward at the mirror. I wonder if she feels as stunning as I think she is.

She says something about a dress with sleeves. I can't focus, I'm overwhelmed by the beauty that the photograph didn't portray accurately at all. She truly is a vision. And she'll be mine. She turns right to exit, and I duck back behind the wall. She walks past me as I press myself deeper into the chair, willing myself to become invisible.

My phone vibrates in my pocket, and I let Penny know I'll be back in a moment before heading outside to take the call.

"What is it, Luca?" I would be irritated, but I shouldn't be here anyway.

"Declan sent over the final paperwork. I'm sending the funds. You sure you want to go through with this, right?" Luca is the youngest of us, and of the four of us, he's by far the most reserved.

"Send it. I have to go. I'll meet you at the office in an hour."

I hang up and sneak back in.

"Look, I love the last one, but if I'm not wearing that, I don't really have a preference..." She's only feet away from me at the counter. I have to duck behind a rack to stay hidden.

Penny tells her she will send the finalized dress to her address, and she makes her way out of the store.

"What was that about?" I ask Penny as I walk up to the front counter.

"It seems your bride is still a little self-conscious about showing her arms, Mr..." she trails off.

"Totaro. Mr. Totaro." I look at the dresses that have been hung on the rack next to her. They are not nearly as glamorous as the dress I saw Devina wearing moments ago.

"I can assure you, she'll still be a beautiful bride, but I wish she had picked the last dress. She was stunning." She sighs.

"Penny, I know there is a quick turnaround on this, but how fast can you add sleeves to the dress she tried on last? I'll pay whatever it costs. Just let me leave a note so she isn't too upset," I say, pulling a wad of cash from my suit pocket.

"Well, I'm sure I can put something together." She beams. "What a lucky girl she is to have a man who loves her this much."

"You have no idea." I smile and count out the total before thanking her again and heading out.

Every ounce of me wants Declan to pay for what he did, but being within a foot of Devina Sullivan rocked me to my core in a way that I can't quite explain. Her striking green eyes, her sultry voice, and the scent of birch wood and lavender lingered in the shop after she left. It's all more than I was prepared for. The combination made me want to reach out and touch her.

The plan is simple. Marry Devina. Make her fall in love with me. Make her sign over her shares of the company. Put a bullet between her eyes. With the Sullivans in my pocket and my father out of the picture, we'll be unstoppable. We'll own this city. In doing so, we'll start taking out the trash that has been making its way past our borders and legitimize more of the unsavory parts of this business.

I pride myself on my ability to obtain whatever I set my mind to. In this case, it's Ms. Sullivan. But as I leave the store and head to the office, the idea of keeping her for my entertainment and pleasure is becoming more enticing than anything. Fortunately, once this arrangement is sealed with a kiss next week, I'll have plenty of time to decide what to do with her...and to her.

# Chapter 5

*Devina*

Sitting at my vanity, I twist a curl between my fingers. Staring back at me is a woman I don't recognize. Soft Copper curls frame my face. I'm wearing more makeup than usual, but Declan let me hire an artist, so it's tastefully done. I look innocent. Pure. It's perfect. No one would ever suspect me as someone who wants to drive a blade through a man's throat and set him on fire.

I run my fingers along my sleeves.

My dress arrived yesterday in a box with a personalized note: *What my wife wants, my wife gets.*

My initial reaction was to call the store and tell Penny she made a mistake, but I knew there wouldn't be enough time to find another dress. How did he know this was the dress I wanted? God, I hope he's not a stalker creep. The independent woman in me wants to bitch about the audacity of this man. There was one single task I had control over—this dress, and he took over that too. One more thing I didn't get to choose for myself. I want to be annoyed, but I'm also in a perfect dress with perfect sleeves that make me feel like a beautiful woman who wasn't maimed by flames.

A text comes through from Taylor.

> **Taylor: Break a leg today**

Me: Will do

Taylor: Not another person's. I just feel like I have to say that.

Me: haha. I know what you meant. Broken legs will come later.

Taylor: I assume you'll be...busy... tonight. Touch base with me tomorrow so we can make some decisions.

Me: Gotcha

I can hear people bustle outside my door, but I know they aren't here for me. Only Declan is here for me. While he believes these nuptials are the cure to maintaining the family business, most of our "family" isn't too keen on being in the same building with who they believe is the enemy. They have no idea that I want more than anything to bring them down and plan to do just that.

Before revenge can be tasted, I need to confirm which Capo is at fault and win him over. It's easier to attack an opponent whose guard is down. And with my timeline, I have to put on the show of my life. It will be my last one, after all.

My lungs constrict as the weight of today becomes heavy. The thought of walking into that room with everyone silently judging me brings on a wave of nerves I wasn't expecting.

I wish Scarlet were here. She would be fixing my veil and giving me advice about pleasing my man. She was always more experienced than I was. After the fire, I had little to no desire or opportunity to meet a man. I didn't just lose a sister that night.

I lost a piece of my heart, and right now, I'm not mourning the girl who was taken under the cover of night. I'm mourning the future that she will never have, the future I have to endure without her.

My mother died when I was three. Scarlet and I only knew her from photos. My father died the night of the fire. He was an abrasive man, just as evil as the man I'm hunting, but I can't help but imagine how different today would be if he were preparing to walk me down the aisle—If we were able to share in a dance.

But I quickly shove those images away, knowing I'm doing this for one reason. I have to stay focused. We have one shot, and I can't afford to miss the target.

I place my hand on my chest, breathing in, *one, two, three, four...*out *one, two, three, four...*

Not a moment later, my door swings open and a man hurries inside. He keeps one hand on the knob and uses the other to close it swiftly but quietly. My eyes snap up, and when he turns to face me, our eyes connect like magnets through the reflection in front of me. Eyes so dark, I could fall in and never hit bottom. He's in a dark gray suit and white shirt. I can see the outline of something drawn on his chest and creeping out from the base of his right sleeve. Instinctively, I pull down on mine. His black straight hair, slightly longer in the front, falls over his forehead, perfectly framing his chiseled jaw. He's about a foot taller than I am, making him well over six feet. He's muscular, but not bulky. His gaze quickly shifts from uncertainty to pure desire as he seems to peer straight into my soul with intensity.

*Fuck.*

# Chapter 6

*Ryder*

"**W**ow," I whispered to myself more than her.

I can see now that the dress was a great choice. She's radiant. The bodice fits her form without being overly snug. The lace, as delicate as she is. The hues of gold complement her auburn hair. She's even more beautiful now with the afternoon sun peering through the stained glass windows. It's as if I'm seeing her for the first time, yet as familiar as coming home.

She sits at her mirror and our eyes are locked through the reflection. For a moment, a wave of déjà vu crashes over me, though I'm not sure I've ever had the privilege of gazing directly into eyes so angelic. I surely would have remembered.

"Did you come for me?" she asked, breaking our silence and standing. Her voice dances across the space between us and straight to places I didn't know still existed in me. "Is it time?" she pushes when I don't answer.

"You must be the bride," I clear my throat, trying to recover.

I wanted to see her before the ceremony, but I hadn't thought about what would happen once I crossed this threshold.

The corner of her mouth perks. "Nothing gets past you," she says almost playfully. "And you are?"

"I'm Ryder. Ryder Totaro."

"Oh, you're Philippe's older brother," she says matter-of-factly and makes her way to the small sofa to sit while she adjusts her sleeves over her wrists. Twice she's done that now.

26

"Uh, yeah. Have you met him?" *Where would she have met Philippe?*

"No, I wanted to wait until the big day." I raise an eyebrow, perplexed by her statement. I think there has been some confusion. "This isn't a traditional marriage, so I figured it doesn't really matter who my betrothed is. He didn't want to see me either," she continues, but there is sadness behind her smile.

She's wrong. I have spent the last six days pining over her. Fighting every urge to see her.

"I don't think your groom didn't want to see you," I assure her. "Six days isn't much time to get your affairs in order before your life changes."

"You're right." She sighs. "Can I tell you something?" Her large green eyes turn cautious. She's testing me.

"Of course." *Fuck, tell me everything just so I can listen to your sweet voice.*

I make my way to the footstool across from her and sit, our knees almost touching.

"I'm about to marry a stranger. In most places on earth, that is completely insane," she babbles on. "But I'm kind of...excited?" she finally confesses, tugging at the sleeves around her wrists. *Three.*

"Is that a question?"

"My sister told me when we were younger that fear is actually excitement, so I sometimes have trouble deciding which one I'm feeling."

I'm an asshole, but I can't let on that I know more than I do. "Is she here? Your sister?"

Her head tilts to the right with an unspoken question. "No. She's gone." Her face becomes unreadable, and she doesn't offer any further explanation.

"That's unfortunate." I mean it. "You get to marry one of the most eligible bachelors in Boston, and you'll carry the Totaro name. There are worse things that could happen." I leaned forward on my elbows, clasping her fidgeting hands in mine. "Welcome to the family." I grin. "We're excited to have you."

"Thanks." She hides a blush, her eyes shifting to avoid mine. "I lost most of my family a long time ago. I'm sure you know my brother, Declan. He's all I have left. I think he's the only person here that I know."

Someone could unknowingly mistake her words for self-pity, but they are laced with a shield of armor. Armor, I hope to one day shatter.

I take a moment to ponder. I should come clean about what is about to happen. But something tells me she needs a reason to laugh. Hell, this entire situation is laughable. Do people arrange-marry each other anymore? Am I any better than a man ordering a wife online? I even paid for her...I wonder if she knows about that.

This will all have to be discussed at another time. "Well, now you know me." I stand and give her a wink. "If you get nervous, just look at me. I promise you won't be up there alone."

She lets out a chuckle, and my breath catches in my throat. A simple melody I didn't know my heart needed. I make a mental note to put all of my secondary priorities on hold until I can find a reason to ruin Ms. Sullivan, because I can't think of anything other than tossing her in a cage and throwing away the key. I want to keep her forever.

"I'll see you out there." She stands, and I give her hands a slight squeeze before letting them go and turning to leave.

"You'll do great, little sparrow." I don't know why I fucking said that, but I left before I could see her reaction.

Now I need to decide if I want to clip her wings or watch her fly.

# Chapter 7

*Devina*

My mind is still reeling from the encounter with Ryder. How odd for him to pay me a visit. He didn't mention anything about his brother. Perhaps he was sent in to catch a glimpse of me and report back to Philippe and Luca. I shouldn't be surprised that his oldest brother didn't make the long trip back to the States for our wedding.

A knock at the door snaps me back to reality. "Vi, can I come in?" Declan opens the door before I answer.

"Well, what do you think?"

His smile doesn't reach his eyes, but he tells me how beautiful I look. I know this is a somber day for us both.

"You don't have to do this. You don't know for sure..." In a building full of opposition, it's not unusual for him not to want to say the rest of his thoughts out loud.

"Look, we all need this, right? This makes everyone happy. You get your alliance, and one lucky Totaro man gets a spicy redhead," I quip.

He shakes his head, refusing to find the humor in this horrific situation.

Producing a black box from his pocket, he takes a deep breath before looking up to the ceiling—praying, perhaps? "Scarlet would have been much better at this than I am, but I thought you should have this. You know, a piece of her."

Inside, her silver Claddagh ring sits cushioned on a satin pillow. Declan had taken it after the fire for safekeeping. The only tangible thing we have left of hers.

"You kept it all this time. Are you sure?"

"You're important to me. I know I don't always make that known. But I need you to keep it. Wear it always." Placing the ring on my right hand, I make that promise.

Music begins and I can hear the ushers requesting our guests to be seated.

"Well, looks like we better get this show on the road," I say as he hands me a bouquet of satin flowers and I take one final look in the mirror.

The sound of the piano reverberates through the building as we exit my suite and make our way toward the grand hall.

With each step I take, my heart beats louder. For a moment, I wonder how bad the consequences would be if I turned left instead of right and made a run for it.

They say when you die, your life flashes in before your eyes, but it's at this moment that a kaleidoscope of emotions and memories flood through my mind. The only memory I have of my mother, chasing the three of us around the garden, before Declan turned into a shell of a person driven by money and power. The image of Scarlet and I jumping on my bed with feather boas and heart-shaped sunglasses, giving my stuffed animals a concert. But they quickly turn dark as I remember the blood that stained her sheets and the vacant look her lifeless body gave me before I was forcefully pulled away from her.

I know I can't turn away. This is the only chance I have to deliver justice. We turn right and pause in front of two large cherry wood doors. This is it.

"Please stand for the bride." The announcement is made and the door swings open.

I haven't been able to choose many things in my life. Each decision from school to friends to where I live and what I do has been chosen for me. Mostly by the men in my life. But not this.

This is my choice.

*I choose this.*

My eyes are closed. *Inhale. One, two, three, four.* Declan pulls me to begin my walk. *Exhale. One, two, three, four.* I open my eyes.

Jet black eyes that look like they want to devour me, meet mine from across the crowded room. My breath is caught in my throat and my mind tries to catch up to me.

The weight of today's ceremony hangs heavy in the air around us, yet I feel like I am floating. If Declan weren't holding my arm, I'm certain I would drift away. My mind finally understands what is happening when we reach the base of the steps leading up to the priest. His strong hand accepts mine from Declan and he pulls me close.

"You?" I whisper as if we're conspiring against everyone in the room.

"Me." Ryder flashes me a sinful smirk and brings the back of my fingers to his lips.

I break our gaze and look past Ryder to his brothers who are serving as groomsmen. Seeing them in the news is nothing compared to real life. I recognize Luca immediately and hide my embarrassment when I see Phillipe, only to look back at a grinning Ryder. Turning to take in the massive room full of people, I can feel my chest begin to tighten and I feel flush.

"Eyes on me, *sparrow*," he demands with a squeeze of my hand and I immediately obey.

It's a relatively short service with a more modern agenda. When it's time for rings, I panic, having no one to hand my bouquet to. He gently takes the satin flowers and hands them to one of the men behind him, who accepts without hesitation.

My face relaxes as we each take our gold bands from the priest and begin our vows. I say each word with intention and promise, but there's a darkness surrounding us. I walked into this with eyes wide open, but for some reason, I feel like I'm selling my soul to the devil.

We speak the remaining vows in unison, somehow entranced by this experience. I'm sure we're not speaking much louder than a whisper as if our oath is meant to be heard only by our souls.

"...Until death do us part," we each conclude.

"You may now kiss your bride," the priest elatedly announces to my husband.

If he can sense my fear, he doesn't show me. He steps toward me, bringing me in close before brushing a loose curl from my cheek. His eyes seem dangerous and owning as he brings his lips to mine. I've traded one sentence for another. The joy and anguish are not lost in the moment, but I can't help but feel like I've been struck by a lightning bolt and the warm sensation pulls deep into my belly as his lips take mine.

He pulls away without a smile. Concern maybe? Can he feel what I'm hiding? His expression is a curious one.

Clapping erupts around us and our attention is demanded by the crowd.

"Good girl, little sparrow," he says, his lips touching the shell of my ear. I have to look away as his words slap me right in my core.

Ryder leads us back down the aisle and to the dressing room as music plays.

I don't know if I'm mad or completely relieved. He's the most handsome of the brothers, but now I felt like the fucking punchline of a joke. I had every intention of getting through today by focusing on the prize. Not a husband, but the sweet taste of revenge as I plant my blade into the neck of the man who took everything from me before making him melt in the same flames he used against us. Now, the most handsome man I've ever seen is holding my hand and dragging me back to a room where we'll be alone. Part of me wonders if I should just start a kill list and add his name to it. The other is telling me to let this man do outrageously dirty things once the door is shut.

"I'm sure you have questions," he begins after shutting the

door.

# Chapter 8

*Ryder*

---

The look in my wife's eyes tells me that she's definitely not
happy. Something draws me to her. I crave her. And after
having tasted her only moments ago, I don't think I'll ever be
able to let her go. So much for my plans of revenge.

She looks at me expectantly. "Part of me wants to slap you."
Somehow, I know she's saying exactly what is on her mind.

"And the other part?" I ask.

"What do you mean the other part?" She walks past me to
place her flowers on the vanity.

"You said 'part of you' wants to slap me. What about the
other part?" I cock a brow, trying to read her as I approach. If she
does try to slap me, I'm sure the sting will bring more pleasure
than pain.

She turns to face me and we're only inches apart. Her eyes
travel north to meet mine. Just as I thought, the sparks that
erupted during our kiss reignite and fizzle beneath the surface,
waiting to explode.

"I-I don't know," she stammers.

Until now, she has appeared to be nothing but concise,
poised, and confident, but the desire to unravel her can't make
me falter. I need to maintain stature. Fighting the urge to devour
her, now I realize breaking her will never be an option. Rather,
keeping her will be my mission. Playing with her will be my new
adventure. Watching as her walls shatter around us, around *me*,
will be the ultimate victory.

I can tell she's hiding something. She's much too eager to

stand her ground and put up a fight, but there's a reservation in her body language that she probably can't tell that I notice. The hesitation in her eyes speaks volumes as I reach up to brush that pesky curl away from her face. God, her breathtaking eyes look like the entrance to the deepest soul I've ever encountered.

"I think I do." I lean in, cradling her dainty face in my palm, ready to consume what is now mine.

I can sense her internal struggle as she blinks, bringing her back to the moment before we're able to get lost in each other.

"I think you don't." She shakes her head and takes a step back. "You think you can just buy me this dress and pick out these flowers, and I'll fawn over you? I'm sorry to be a disappointment, Mr. Totaro, but I'm not one of the women you pick up at one of your clubs." Her legs meet the stool behind her as she continues to back away from me until she's forced to sit.

"*Mrs. Totaro.*" I retreat a step to give her space. "I can assure you, I was never under the impression that you were one of those women. From what I've seen, you're well-spoken and aren't shy about saying what's on your mind. You're elegant but insecure about something. Hence, your decision to pick a much less flattering dress than you wanted. But you go after what you want. I doubt it was your brother's idea for you to enter into this agreement, and yet, here you are."

A quiet gasp leaves her lips. I've struck a chord.

"How did you know about my dress?" Her eyes squint daggers at me.

I cross my arms, considering how much I want her to know. "I know a lot of things, little sparrow. What I don't know is how you take your coffee in the morning." I step closer and hold a hand out to her. A request. She accepts, and I guide her up to me. "I don't know what you love and what you fear." I run my fingers down both of her arms as she stands radiantly before me. I feel her shiver under me. "And I don't know why I feel like you're hiding something... but I can't wait to know it all."

A knock at the door turns both of our heads. *Dammit.* I forgot we have the rest of the wedding traditions to tackle.

When we turn back, she has composed herself, and again, I'm unable to read her. She steps out of her white heels and walks over to the sofa to sit before pulling a pair of white Converse shoes out of a bag.

"Black with sugar." She slips one shoe on. "Fire." She slips on the other and stands. "And I'm not hiding anything," she states as she walks toward me and raises her chin defiantly.

"You love or fear fire?" I ask.

After contemplating her answer for a moment, she simply replies, "Both."

She's an odd one, but one who is quickly becoming my new obsession. "Well, I don't know how far we've gotten, but I'm pretty sure we're far enough away from you wanting to slap me that we can go enjoy the rest of our wedding." I give her my most charming smile.

She laughs, her hand reaching up to my arm, sending a shock down my spine. "Don't do that! Oh my God, please never do that again."

She sees the confusion on my face.

"Look, I don't want this to come off the wrong way, but that cheesy smirk is not going to win me over." She chuckles. "If that was your intention, I mean."

And just like that—I'm thoroughly embarrassed. I'm Ryder *fucking* Totaro. Women love me. Throw their panties at me, love me. But my wife, this five-and-a-half-foot woman—if I'm being generous—is standing in front of me making me feel like a love-sick puppy who just got a newspaper swat to the nose.

Seeing her in the store, talking to her earlier, watching her float down the aisle...she was a vision of grace. Her actions are sweet and meek. But clearly, I was wrong. This woman is full of fire. The fire she both loves and hates.

I have a feeling I'll enjoy trying to figure her out.

# Chapter 9

*Devina*

I'm almost certain I just insulted my new husband. Not my intention. But how else was I supposed to react? He's obviously full of himself. I've been railroaded by men my whole life. First, my father, who made the laws we were bound to, then my brother, who was forced to take on the role as my caregiver and isn't shy about letting me know how he feels about it.

But I chose this.

I. Chose. This.

I need to calm down before I do something stupid. This can't all be for nothing.

"Look, I'm sorry." I sigh. "I'm just really overwhelmed. Today is...a lot. I'm not usually so outspoken."

He seems to be sympathetic to my apology and raises his hands gently in defeat. "No problem. I get it. Today is a lot for us both. We have to make an appearance at our own reception, but we can leave whenever you want and go home."

*Home.*

I'll be going to a new home tonight with a stranger. A ping of doubt rumbles deep in my gut, but his pleading eyes tell me his kindness is genuine.

"I bet everyone is dying to meet the happy couple," I quip and hold my hand out to him. A truce.

He takes it and runs his thumb over my knuckles. "We can be, you know?"

"Can be what?"

He smiles. No sly grin. An honest smile that makes its way up to his dark eyes. "Happy."

Maybe he's right. I might as well try to be happy for now. It's not like I'll be murdering anyone tonight. I'm in a white dress and will soon be surrounded by a few hundred people. What's the harm in smiling for a few pictures and eating some cake? Hell, I'll even dance with him if he asks.

He seems like the type who would ask. Although I'm not sure if it will be because he wants to or because he's obligated to. I'm also not sure I care as long as his hands make their way to my body.

I can't deny how attractive he is. I'm pretty sure I'm extremely excited for all the other things he may consider to be obligatory later...in the dark...when we're alone.

But for now, I need to keep my mind focused and my legs closed.

*Seriously Devina?*

The reception hall is even grander than the church. Our time in the bridal suite must have taken longer than I realized. The entry to the hall is littered with guests, and they part like the Red Sea for us as we make our way toward the doors.

"What's the code word?" he whispers to me.

"Code word?"

"When you're ready for it to be over. You know, code word." He shrugs.

I chuckle to myself. Nothing about him screams *king of the underworld*.

"What about 'fly'?" I ask.

"Perfect, little sparrow. Perfect." He squeezes my hand twice, and I watch as he skillfully slides his mask in place. He's the leader of this pack, and I'm reminded that as his wife, I must also carry myself in the same regal manner.

The pessimist in me takes a mental note that his earlier kindness was likely to gain my compliance. I'm not sure why, though, I did not indicate that I would cause a scene. But I guess our mutual lack of trust is just about the only thing we have in common right now.

"Eyes on me," he reminds me as we make our grand entrance into the hall that is already filled with hundreds of people.

I look up to meet his stare, and a flash of genuine adoration crosses his face before quickly being replaced by the stone-cold killer I know he and most of the men here are. As we make our way to our table, his wall is up completely, and I can't help but worry that I may end up running headfirst into that wall at some point.

I still can't tell which part of him is *him*, or if he's even shown me yet. He's been a perfect gentleman so far, pulling out my chair and planting a kiss on my forehead before excusing himself to speak to the guards to our right. I should be grateful that this ruthless Totaro man seems pleased enough with me to be nice, even trying to crack a few jokes and taking a genuine interest in me. But this also poses the issue that my mind is now equally weighing thoughts of murder and the anticipation of his hands being everywhere—anywhere—on me.

An orchestra plays in the corner, and couples make their way to the dance floor to sway. The dim lights create a romantic environment while waiters pass by the tables with champagne. White linen drapes over the tables, and white lilies stand in tall vases. I love lilies, but they are meant for funerals, not weddings.

*Focus Vi.*

The Cap I desperately need to find has to be here. Everyone who is anyone is.

My racing thoughts are brought to an abrupt halt. I smell him before I see him. A chill shoots down my spine. Whiskey and cigar smoke poorly coated with mint. A combination I will never forget. The scent wraps around me like a noose, and my back straightens. I'm frozen, but I try my best to mask my fear, hatred, and rage.

There are a million ways I envisioned meeting this man face to face, yet I feel so unprepared. If my fists become any tighter, I may draw blood. I look down at the steak knife to my right and wonder how mad Declan would be if I used it. With one swift movement, I could grab it and slice his throat before he even knew what was happening. They'd probably kill me, but I'm so close to death, I'd take her hand willingly as she carries me to the other side.

"Ah, there you are," Ryder's voice penetrates through my racing thoughts. I turn to him to stand, hoping to meet his gaze, without grabbing the knife. Instead, he turns me fully around, and I'm face to face with the man from my nightmares. "Devina, please meet my father, Nico Totaro."

My skin prickles. My blood runs cold, yet I allow the corners of my mouth to turn up in a pleasant smile.

"Pleasure to meet your bride, son." He takes my hand in his and brings it to his face to imitate the gesture of a kiss. I fight the bile slowly making its way up my chest and throat. "No need to be formal now, they call me Cap." He shoots me a slimy grin. Perhaps if you didn't know he was such a murderous prick, you could consider him good-looking. I know Scarlet did.

Knowing that I have a terrible poker face, I try my best to look away and step closer to Ryde. I keep my smile, knowing it doesn't meet my eyes.

Fate allows me the courtesy of a quick getaway when the speakers call for the bride and groom to the dance floor. It's time for our first dance.

"We'll catch up with you later, Cap. I have a bride to win over right now." He takes my hand, looking curiously at me as he guides me to the center of the room, where people have created a circle for us. He has already accused me of keeping secrets, and anxiety settles deep in my chest that I've just raised another red flag.

"*Luminary*" by Joel Sunny is played by the small orchestra in the corner.

"I hope you don't mind I chose this without you." Ryder

spins me with one hand before bringing me in close.

"There are no words." I raise a brow. "And you've chosen everything without me."

"The best moments in your life should leave you searching for them and coming up empty," he says, ignoring my second statement.

What an odd thing to say. "Words are important to me."

"I gathered that earlier today." He chuckles, probably remembering how quickly I can spew word vomit. In truth, I've learned that spoken words are often a load of crap, but the written ones...those are priceless to me. Something that can be treasured forever.

He guides me around the floor like a professional. The tempo increases, and I spot a movement from the crowd, causing my eyes to falter, along with my feet.

"Eyes on me," he demands gently.

He spins me, towers above me, and looks so deep into me that everything and everyone begins to fade away. It's just us now. His large hand spans across the small of my back, holding me closer than I've ever been to a man. I feel out of breath, but I know that if this next is my last, I will be caught by his embrace. An embrace that holds so much electricity it could surely bring me back to life.

The last note causes an abrupt stop, and I realize he is breathing at my tempo, chests rising and falling rapidly. I desperately wish to be alone with him. My expectations for tonight sprint to the forefront of my mind, and as nervous as I am to be completely exposed, I want nothing more than to feel him in me as soon as possible.

He gently releases me but keeps my eyes hostage as he smiles ever so slightly, a playful tension growing. His fingers drop slowly to the edge of my sleeve before he gives it a gentle tug. He has seen me do this enough to know I wouldn't want to show my arms. A subtle confession that he knows more about me than I do about him. I realize that at some point soon, I'll have to let him see all of me.

Gentle applause erupts around us. The crowd taps their glasses for us to kiss.

"You don't have to—" I begin, but his lips are on me and his hand glides up around my neck, creeping up toward the nape of my hair.

His tongue whispers against my bottom lip, and I open for him, deepening our kiss. No one would suspect we met only hours ago. I would never have suspected that a mafia heathen could hold me so tenderly with the same hands he uses to kill people.

It all becomes too much. I shouldn't be confused right now. I should be putting on the best show of my life so I can go out with a bang—or a flame, rather. But I'm not acting when I lean into him and wrap my arm under his jacket and around his waist, bringing him as close as he can be. I need it to stop. I need to stop.

I break away gently, looking up into eyes that can see everything I'm trying to hide, and I know it's time to go before I trip and fall.

Swallowing down the butterflies threatening to escape, I have no choice but to get out while I'm ahead.

With a gentle breath, which is all I can muster, I let the word leave my lips, "Fly."

# Chapter 10

*Ryder*

⑈⑈⑈ Smells Like Teen Spirit — Stevie Howie ⑈⑈⑈

Gratitude rushed through me when Devina gave the code word to leave. After our second kiss, there was nothing I wanted more than to take her home and claim every part of her that she tried so hard to hide.

There was no way she didn't feel what I felt. The way our lips ignited, the ease of our caresses, the desire to explore each other. It was all too loud to ignore.

She didn't have to ask twice. Leading her with my hand on the base of her back, we made our way out to a waiting car.

Leaning to get in with her, I feel the vibration of my phone in my suit jacket. It's Ronnie.

"This better be good, it's my wedding night, you know." I try not to sound irritated, but I am. He wouldn't call if it wasn't important. Devina turns to me, her eyes squint in an attempt to translate my reaction.

"Russians, Boss. We have a lead, and it needs to be dealt with now before they change locations again. It took two weeks to nail them down this time," he explains.

Knowing I have to leave Devina makes me physically aching in all the worst ways. But this is part of the job. She must understand, considering who her father was and who her brother is.

"Ten minutes," I nearly bark as I hang up and pocket my phone. How do you tell your bride that you are ditching her on your wedding night? I don't want to assume I know where this would have gone, but judging by our last interaction, I feel like she wants me as much as I want her. However, she's hesitant to admit it.

"You have to go." Her shoulders pull back slightly as if she were adjusting a new barrier that I will have to deconstruct.

"Yes. I don't want to. This is the worst timing." I run my hand through my hair. "This is a job we've been working on for a while, and Declan will need to join us."

Her eyes become distant. "Look, this isn't real, right? This is an arrangement." Something about the way she drags out the words makes my stomach churn. "A business arrangement? You aren't bound to me, Ryde. I'll see you...at home."

She's being too gracious about this. But perhaps she's right. This is an arrangement. We both have our obligations in and outside of this marriage. Right now, mine is to find out what these guys are transporting and get them out of our territory. It's the reason her brother sought an alliance with us to begin with. He simply didn't have the manpower to accomplish the task.

I pull her closer to me by her hips until she is nearly on my lap. Her quick inhale of surprise makes me smile. "The staff will get you settled. Rest, take a bath, eat, read, whatever you want, it's yours. Fiona will help get you settled." I twist that pesky curl near her face. "I'll be back before dinner tomorrow, little sparrow."

My new business partner, as she would consider herself, is staring at me with muted disappointment. She either isn't used to showing emotion, or she's exceptionally good at disguising it.

"Will you be okay?" There's a part of me that wants to be reckless, but she nods and rests her hand on my chest, permitting me to leave.

*Permission.* Like I'm a fucking child. Me. Ryder Totaro, asking for his wife's permission. I never thought I'd see this day.

I wonder if she even knows the effect she's having on me.

But we don't have much time to consider such things. I kiss her forehead and adjust her back in the seat next to me before sliding out of the car.

My heart sinks as I watch the car away in the direction of our home. A home she doesn't know. A home she'll have to enter for the first time without me.

I have to get back to her as soon as possible.

We had a lead on where the Russians were keeping their new merchandise, and I have to chase that down.

I pull up to a worn-down brick building and wait for Declan. I'm sure he's just as eager as I am to get these assholes out of our territory, but tonight is not about starting a war. It's about gathering information. We need to know what they're pushing and who knows. It may be something I need and can leverage. Maybe there will be more than one way for me to screw Declan Sullivan over.

He pulls up in his obnoxious sedan. I guess I'm not one to talk as I secure my helmet on the side of my bike. We're both still in our wedding attire.

"Ryder," he grunts in acknowledgment.

"Declan."

"Let's get this over with."

"You read my mind."

We walk a block to the back of the building. Peering around the corner, I see two men waiting by the large steel door. I reach my hand back to stop Declan. Looking over his left shoulder, he sends a questioning nod up toward the fire escape, and I return one in agreement.

Luckily, the window on the second floor is open enough for us to squeeze through. Hidden behind a stack of wooden crates, we look down to see ten women shackled by their necks and wrists. Seven men stand guard as they cower in a circle.

Declan and I look at each other, knowing that there's no way we would be able to take on this situation without the help of our crews.

A man with bright blonde hair enters the room, barking orders. "Get them to the dock. The ship is already waiting. Crate 71459 will be left open for you. Boat leaves in an hour."

The men grab the chains and begin to escort the women out of the room and into the truck that is waiting in the alley.

Declan is halfway out the window when I turn around. I'm on his heels quickly to ensure he doesn't try something stupid. Once we scale the fire escape back to the ground floor, we take a quick scan of the area and head back to the vehicles.

"This is worse than I thought." I pinch my fingers over the bridge of my nose. "If we call everyone now, we can meet at the dock and take them out."

"There's no time for that tonight, Ryder. We might make it, but the whole crew? They won't make it on time."

"Those are fucking *women*." I stop in my tracks baffled that he's not as enraged as I am after what we just witnessed. "Like your fucking sister, Declan, my *wife*. Are you seriously going to waste time arguing about this with me?" I seethe.

He lets out a pained sigh. His indecisiveness is making my skin crawl, and it takes all of my energy not to shoot him in the face right now before I go take care of business. "I'll call in a few on the way. You better have a plan in mind by the time we get there. I'm not going in blind." He walks past me toward his car.

My helmet is on and I'm already gearing up to leave when he turns back to approach me with a pointed finger. "And don't ever bring up my sister again. I would do anything for her. Even let her marry your dumb ass."

"Was that for her? Or was that for *you*?"

His stare turns ice cold, and his fists clench before we part ways.

We might hate each other, but we have a common enemy, which tends to bring people together.

The streets are consistently occupied with people who have no idea about the workings of the underground happenings that take place. Weaving in and out of traffic gives me a few minutes on Declan, and I'm grateful for the space between us. I still can't seem to understand why he was so willing to give his sister away. According to him, he did it for her. What could she possibly be gaining from this marriage?

I call Luca and Philippe on my headset, and they're both within ten minutes of the docks. Breaking every speed limit to beat our crew to the location, I try to outpace the thoughts of the women we found shackled and broken.

Parking and jumping off my bike, I wait the five minutes it takes for Declan and his crew to arrive and park their cars in the shadows. We don't have a lot of force, but there's enough to put up a decent fight. If anything, the Russians will know we're onto them and maybe even scare them away. Who am I kidding? We're about to start a war.

I dole out positions for everyone, and before we split, Declan hands me a wooden box. "A bomb. Nothing too big, but if shit gets too crazy, it'll be a good distraction."

"Are you seriously trying to make your sister a widow already? I'm not taking this."

"Oh, let me." Luca is all too eager. I roll my eyes, but hand it over.

"You just drive around with a bomb on you all the time? Did you have that at my wedding?" I give Declan a curious look.

"Maybe one of us has underestimated the other," he replies over his shoulder as he steps away. "Don't worry, it's just a small one," he cuts back at me.

"Okay, gents, it's go time," Ronnie announces.

One by one, we pursue the guards. It only takes two falling for the rest to begin returning fire. "Don't hit the container!" I remind our men.

Shots ring out, and blood-curdling screams echo from inside the metal box. One of the Russians ducks behind the pallets to the right and makes a run for it, but Philippe lets out a hefty chuckle as he begins his pursuit.

We approach the container door. "We're here to help you," I

announce to the women in a quiet voice with my hands slightly raised. It's then that I realize they aren't women. They're girls. Young girls. The oldest is likely fifteen or so.

A chill makes its way down my spine, remembering that Declan wanted to leave them—the heartless bastard.

"Keys," Luca says in a hushed tone before tossing me the ring, and I begin unlocking the padlocks around their necks.

"Let's get out of here. Declan, have your men bring them to a hospital and text me when it's done."

"Will do, *boss.*" God, this guy is a bigger prick than I thought.

"We have a problem." Luca looks back at us and announces as three SUVs speed into the parking lot.

"Luca, get the girls out of here. Give me the bomb," I order.

He holds out the box, and I grab it as gently as I can. Guns, no problem. Knives, I want them all. But I have no experience with bombs, and I have no idea how much damage they can do.

Shots begin just as Luca reaches the fence of the container yard and hastily ushers the girls into one of Declan's vans before speeding away. Now I'm here alone, and all I have is this damn bomb.

I set it and slide it as far as I can into the container before making a run for cover. My heart is beating so hard I can feel it in my ears. Time slows as I run toward my bike. The faint click behind me lets me know I've run out of time. I'm chased by a loud bang and heat pulsating at my back. While the men who arrived late to the party are a fair enough distance away, I can't seem to get far enough away with the gravel sliding under my shoes.

Declan's little distraction was larger than I thought. Flames lick at my neck, and I'm forced to dive. There's no way for me to escape the aftermath now. Just as I brace myself for the impact, a piece of metal meets the back of my skull, and everything goes black before I feel my body hit the concrete.

# Chapter 11

## *Ryder*

*M*y mind is in a haze. Everything hurts.

I can see her. Michaela. Her raven hair is skewed across the pillow, and a needle is still in her vein. Overdose.

I feel the weight of Cap's palm hit my shoulder, and he gives a comforting squeeze, but I'm numb. He hangs his head, not knowing what to say. There's nothing to say. The lamp on the nightstand is tipped over. Several small bags line its surface. A prominent green stamp lets me know where they come from.

My teeth clench as I try to contain my rage. Declan Sullivan. He did this.

The sound of my father's footsteps retreats, but I can't take my eyes off her. My feet are planted on the filthy carpet of the seedy motel room.

I reach out to feel her cheek. Her skin is still warm. We were too late, but only by minutes. I should be chasing after him. I should peel his skin from his muscles just to hear his screams of agony before shooting him up with the poison he gave to my sweet Michaela.

I know Cap is calling this in right now, and the cops we keep on payroll will have this swept under the rug. His words fade around me as a steady beep grows louder between my ears. *I can't let anyone know I was here. I'll be the likeliest suspect.*

*Beep.*

But he will pay. I'll make him pay.

*Beep.*

# Chapter 12

*Ryder*

I wake in a familiar room.

The consistent beep of a machine next to me brings me back. A sterile scent is in the air, and the lights are dim. *Not a hospital.*

"It's about time you joined us, Mr. Totaro," a familiar voice greets me. Nathan, the family doctor. Not our family, but still.

"What happened? How long have I been out?"

"Two days." He comes closer to wrap something around my arm, and pressure builds. "You have a concussion. I gave you something for the pain, but you'll need to take it easy for a few more days," he instructs.

Pieces of the past few nights play like a movie in my mind until I rewind back enough to remember her. Devina. She has no idea where I am.

Fuck, I have to get home.

Looking down, I realize I'm covered in dirt and blood. I reach for my phone on the desk next to the bed. A message from Luca lets me know that the young women were all taken to the hospital and would be cared for. With all of the connections we have in this city, the staff would be discreet.

"How did I get here?" I ask, remembering everyone leaving me.

"That would be me," Declan answers as he enters the room with two mugs full of coffee. "You didn't think I'd really let my sister become a widow already, did you?"

I chuckle. Maybe he isn't a complete monster. But *maybe* isn't enough to stop me from hating him.

# Chapter 13

*Devina*

**Seven years ago.**

The two lines appear immediately, almost mocking us.

"You're going to run off and marry someone and leave me, Scarlet."

I've never known my sister to be anything less than a hopeless romantic. She's three years older than me and equipped with everything necessary to land any man. Not that *any* man would do. She has her standards high. But this one is different. So different, in fact, that she won't tell me who he is.

I know he's older. Old enough to make her hesitant.

We sit on the bathroom floor with the stick still wet from her urine. In that moment I know our lives would be changing and the idea makes me want to puke. I was angry when Scar first told me she needed me to help her. I wanted so desperately to attend Jessica's sleepover, to finally be included...maybe even have my first kiss with Russell Crowe. We shared four classes together for the past two years and he started showing interest over the past few months.

As much as I enjoy the prospect of Russell's lips on mine, I know she needs me and I will always yield to her. The anger dissipated when she pulled the pregnancy test out from the small brown bag.

"Are you going to tell him?"

"Of course I'm going to tell him, Vi," she says, rolling her eyes at me.

"Fucking great, Scar." I spit, not intending for it to come out as venomous as it did. "Don't you want to go to school and travel? What about everything we planned?"

She's nineteen. She could do whatever she wanted. Unfortunately, I'm stuck here for another two years. As soon as my time is up here, we'd bid farewell to our Irish family and the trouble it brings us. We'd get the hell out of Boston and see the world. We'd move across the globe so quickly, they would never find us.

"We were already planning on getting married, Vi. He wants me forever." I can't help but roll my eyes in an attempt to cover up the sting of betrayal as she swoons.

"You need to tell me who he is. Is he dangerous? Is that why you won't tell me? Oh God, it's not one of Dad's goons is it?" I scrunch my face.

"I won't tell you because he's older and once everyone knows, I'm sure Dad is going to flip out. No one will be happy. I love you Vi, but you are the worst liar in the world. I can't risk it until I'm ready." She isn't wrong. I am the worst liar.

She plans to see him and tell him the "good news" tonight.

I wait in my bed staring up at the ceiling. Obviously, I know how this happened, but *how could this happen*? My room still has pink walls and my shelves are lined with trinkets from my childhood. God, *I* am a baby. I chuckle to myself. Maybe I'll get a room makeover out of this whole ordeal. They'll have to make a nursery, right?

I hear Scarlet's feet pat along the porch and her bedroom window slowly open and close. I make my way over to her room and crawl into bed with her.

"Scar, how did it go?" I break our silence.

"It didn't. We're done." I freeze, never expecting this to be one of the outcomes. "He already has kids and doesn't want another. What am I going to do Vi?" She sobs into her pillow.

"We'll be okay, Scar. We'll do all the things we planned. Nothing will change," I assure her while I rub her back.

"Everything will change, Vi. I'll have a baby now." Her excitement from earlier is gone and replaced with a type of devastation I have yet to experience in my short life. "You'll have to do it all for both of us."

I pet her hair to soothe her, but I'm only a child myself, and I have no idea what the fuck *we* are going to do. Everything in me wants to run. I crave freedom deep in my bones. But do I want it enough to leave her?

I stay until her sobs become fewer and she finally falls asleep. Love seems to make you do the dumbest things. Freedom, I'll chase it. Adventure, I'll run toward it excitedly. Love? No thanks.

I slip out of the covers and make my way back to my room. Closing my eyes, I try to imagine what type of man would turn away a woman so devoted and so full of life—especially since the life she's filled with now is part of him. I don't get too far into my thoughts before the first shot rings out. I stiffen, not knowing if it is one of my dad's men or an attack.

Shots fire outside, and the front door crashes open before footsteps pound up the stairs. *This is an attack.* I slip out of my bed, placing the covers back in place before I grab my baseball bat and stand at attention behind my door. Light filters below the door. A shadow briefly pauses before continuing to Scarlet's room next door. I'm frozen in place. My shallow breath opposes my rapid thoughts and thundering heartbeat.

Two shots.

I don't hear the drop of a body. She was already in bed.

Another set of feet makes their way up the stairs but pauses at the top of the landing.

"I got the old man. Are you done? We have to go, the fire is picking up," a man's voice rumbles.

"There is one more," the first man says.

My breath hitches, and I will myself to be invisible.

"She's not supposed to be here," the second man replies.

Slowly, my doorknob turns and opens only inches, just enough to see my made bed. His strong scent makes my stomach turn, and his shadow lets me know that he's large enough to take me easily, even if I struggle.

"Cap, the fire. Let's go. No one else is here."

The door shuts, and I sink slowly to the floor as their footsteps descend the stairs.

I don't know how long I sat and waited, afraid they were still in the house, but it was long enough for the smoke to reach me. Black clouds drift under the door, and I feel the heat on the other side. I couldn't leave without seeing her. They could have missed. She could be waiting for me.

I stumble to put on my tennis shoes and slip out my window to crawl on the roof above the porch to Scar's side of the house. The flames begin to scorch the door as I frantically pull back the crimson blankets to expose the shots embedded in her torso. The sharp scent of copper stuns me, but I'm quickly brought back to the present when I see her nearly vacant eyes blink.

"You came for me."

"Oh God, Scar, hold on, I can hear help coming," I plead as I try to put pressure on her wounds as sirens blare outside the window.

Scar is everything I'm not. She's the brave one. She convinced me when we were younger that I could jump out of airplanes and climb the highest mountains. When I was eight, we stood on the roof looking over at the swimming pool. "I'm scared, Scar," I had said. "You feel those butterflies in your tummy?" she'd asked. I nodded. "You're not scared, you're excited." Her mischievous smile had stretched to her eyes, and she grabbed my hand. We'd jumped together, and I'd loved every second. But this, this is fear. Consuming, paralyzing fear.

The house begins to collapse around me as the firetrucks finally arrive, and the voices of men travel through the open window. I need to snap out of it, but I want to take her with me. I can't leave without her.

Her hand falls limp in my own, and a single breath leaves

her chest. Disappointment washes over me when it doesn't rise again.

Strong arms wrap around my waist and drag me back. I reach for her, but someone is pulling me, and I lose grip of her arm. Pulling at her fingers, her ring slips off with ease, having been covered in her blood. Time rushes past me and slows all at once, and I'm dragged out the window and placed in the arms of a waiting man.

I want to scream. I want to fight back. I want to be there with her. Everything was taken. Let the fire take me too. I have nothing left.

Sitting with paramedics, I watch as my childhood home burns to ashes. Everything in me, on me, is numb. Shock has taken hold of every atom in my body. I didn't even feel the fire that had crept up my left hand and melted my skin. Help came just in time.

"You're lucky we got to you in time," the man says as he wraps temporary bandages around my arm before telling me I'd be taken to the hospital in a few moments.

I'm screaming in my head, but my ears are ringing, and he seems unaffected by my rage.

I look down at my clenched fist. Opening it, I find Scar's Claddagh ring singed by the heat and caked in dry blood. The tears come quickly, and because she isn't here to lend comfort, I find none. Absolutely none.

I will find who did this, and they will pay with blood. *The Cap* will pay.

*I'll do it for both of us, Scar.*
*I'll be coming for you, Cap.*

# Chapter 14

*Devina*

᭯᭯᭰᭰᭰᭰ When I'm Like This — Kathleen Regan ᭯᭯᭰᭰᭰᭰

Another night, another nightmare. I'm torn between wanting to preserve pieces of that night and wanting to forget it all together. But those memories are the last ones I have of my sister.

I lie in bed, eyes closed, and I welcome the dark thoughts that always follow the nightmare I can't seem to forget. Death. She's waiting for me. I can end it now. I wonder how I would do it. A slash to the wrist, the swallow of one too many pills. I'd tie a rope, but I don't know how, and I don't think you're supposed to Google these things. I try not to spend too much time thinking about killing myself each morning, but the thought is always there. *I can end it all now.* If I do, will Scarlet be disappointed when I meet her on the other side? Maybe I'm a coward. Maybe I'm delusional in my confidence when I think of killing the most dangerous man I could ever face. But my thoughts stray when I wonder how my new husband would react to my death, the death that will come whether I accept it or take it intentionally.

*I'll be back before dinner tomorrow.*

His words ring in my head as I open my eyes in an unfamiliar room, and I have to remind myself where I am.

I'm swimming in blankets that hold his scent and I remember that I made my way into his room last night. I didn't *miss* him. I was lonely. Turning on the television, the news reports a bombing downtown and the recovery of several women who claimed to be victims of a human trafficking ring. Suddenly I feel like a terrible person for wallowing in this huge house just because my husband has been away for a few days.

Three days, to be exact.

No text. No call. No messenger pigeon. Only silence. The house manager, Fiona, has no information for me. I initially hesitated to ask for any updates on the whereabouts of my husband because the last thing I wanted anyone to think was that he was indifferent to me. Yes, we're married. But I reminded him before his departure that this is basically a business transaction. For all I know, he could be nestled breast-deep in one of the women he found prowling around one of his clubs. Not that I care. I don't.

Arrangement. *A business transaction, Devina.* That's what this is.

Still, I can't help but be totally pissed that I didn't even get a courtesy call. I consider calling Declan, but I'm not sure he'll respond as a jealous big brother or hold strong to some kind of male code of honor.

When I first arrived at the estate, I was greeted by Fiona and shown to a room adjacent to the master. If I didn't know better, I would have assumed it was the master suite. The large bed was situated between two tall windows that allowed the sunlight to wake me on my first morning without Ryder.

My first task as a newlywed was to shoot Taylor a quick message explaining that we had the wrong brother and requesting a thorough investigation of the one I married. He said he would call me as soon as it was ready, but two days have passed, and I've received no news. Maybe Taylor will discover that Ryder is a horrible man who kills innocent people and kicks puppies. If he is, I will feel a lot less guilty about killing his father.

I want to hate them all, but I also can't stop thinking of our last kiss. Maybe it's all in my head. I haven't kissed a man in so long, I'm probably romanticizing the entire experience.

I spent the better part of the past two days wandering around the house and trying to settle into the room I was given before finally deciding to retreat to Ryder's room—*our room*. I've never lived with a man—aside from my brother, of course. I also didn't have a full staff to take care of chores and errands. What exactly does one do all day when everything is done for you? Somehow, I'm lonelier in a house full of people than I have ever been living with Declan, who was always gone.

The door leading to the basement was locked, along with Ryder's office. Knowing that anything helpful to my cause would probably be in that room, I reluctantly put my plan on hold and decided to familiarize myself with the staff and my new home.

I roll around in the blankets and will myself to sit up. I can't wither away here. I need to keep up my strength. I need to go for a run.

Tossing my gown on the floor and slipping on a pair of leggings and a comfortable hoodie from the suitcase I'm still living out of, I make my way down the stairs and toward the front door and make a mental note to unpack the one bag of items I brought with me.

"Well, good morning Mrs. Totaro!" Fiona beams. "I was beginning to worry, it's nearly noon."

"Please call me Devina, Fiona. We've been over this." Sitting on the bottom step, I tug on my sneakers. "Any chance my husband will be making an appearance today?"

She nodded at my request. Again. Although I doubt she'll call me by my name. "Mr. Totaro should be home this afternoon. I just received word from his office."

"Great, glad he thought enough of me to check in." I fight the urge to roll my eyes. "I'm going for a run. I won't be long."

"You should bring Sal with you. Mr. Totaro won't like you venturing off on your own," she warns, as kindly as one can when they're ordering you to bring a babysitter.

I open the door to leave. "It's fine, I'll be okay." Dismissing her request, I bolt before anyone can stop me.

The long driveway leads to the main road, which takes me to a small town after about twenty minutes. I'm not sure where I am at first, but I know I'm north of the city. Historic shops line the street and I stumble upon a darling coffee house. A hanging wood sign reads 'Toppers Coffee & Co." Just what I need to start my day.

A glass display case holds drool-worthy donuts and the menu is written on a black chalkboard. Five tables are scattered with an assortment of mismatched chairs that somehow all match perfectly. I instantly feel at home.

I order a cappuccino and pull my burner out to call Taylor.

He picks up on the first ring. "Hey sis."

"Really? 'Hey, sis'? After radio silence for two days?" I don't even try to hide how annoyed I am. The men in my life are driving me crazy and poor Taylor will be receiving the brunt of my bad mood.

"Look, I jumped down a rabbit hole, but I think you'll be pretty happy with what I've found."

I make my way to a table near the window and settle in with my coffee, ready for all of Taylor's tea. "Hit me."

"Well, someone on their side is nearly as good as I am. Files were a bitch to hack into," he begins. "But I was able to get into the legitimate side of their business. Looks like your man has three clubs in the city. There are several more throughout the country and some less exciting businesses. I found an email between the brothers. Apparently, Cap wasn't keen on leaving his life's work in the hands of four bachelors, which I assume is what prompted your arrangement."

"Fine by me." I shrug. "I don't care why he wanted to get married. I'm just glad the opportunity presented itself when it did. I don't need anything on Ryder. I need to know how to get to Cap."

"I know you don't care about your husband's past, but the rabbit hole—" He continues. "Ryder was engaged three years ago. It was announced in the papers."

"If he was already getting married, something must have happened."

"That's for sure. Listen to this. The same woman from the engagement announcement, Michaela Druthers, was found dead in a hotel room with a needle in her arm. This is about six weeks after the engagement."

"Holy shit. That's devastating." I sympathize with Ryder's loss, but I wonder if he's still grieving this woman. Maybe that's why he's stayed away.

"Something is off about it, but I can't put my finger on it. This woman looks so familiar. I know I've seen her before."

"I hate when that happens. Send me a picture and I'll see if I know her." *No, I'm not being nosey about my husband's dead ex.* A ping comes through, and I open the photo only to see someone I never thought I'd see again.

"Tay, this is Hannah." My mind is trying to pull the pieces together.

"Hannah! That's right!" he agrees and I can hear him snap his fingers over the line. "How is Hannah...Michaela Druthers?"

Hannah was Declan's girlfriend until she ghosted him. Well, no pun intended, I guess. I never got the whole story, but I was certain he was going to marry her one day. Two years together and then 'poof' she was gone, and Declan didn't want her name spoken around him again.

Was Hannah cheating on Declan, or was Michaela cheating on Ryder?

"This is definitely weird, but I don't know if it helps us at all. I need info on the target, Tay. Text me tomorrow and keep me posted."

I know I need to get back. Someone is bound to be looking for me. Distracted, I stand and turn right into a woman holding two coffees.

"Oh my gosh, I'm so sorry!" I'm mortified and she's got coffee down the front of her dress.

She chuckles and sets her half-empty cups on the table. "Man, that sucks, but it's all good."

I grab some napkins from the creamer stand and hand them to her. "I wasn't paying attention. I can pay for your dry cleaning," I offer.

"Really, don't worry about it." Her smile tells me she means that. "I'm MaryClaire. I come to this coffee shop every morning and I've never seen you."

"Devina. You can call me Vi." I shake her hand and take her wet napkins to toss in the trash. "Can I at least get you another order? I feel terrible."

"My uncle owns this coffee shop, so I'll just use my 'niece card'." She gives me a wink. "But hey, you look like you have 'new to town' written all over you. Do you want to sit with me?" She nods over to a table on the other side of the room filled with notebooks and a laptop.

"Actually, I have to get home. I'm pretty sure my husband will be looking for me soon."

"Well, maybe another time. Like I said, I usually make a stop here at least once a day. I'll give you my number." She takes out a notebook and scribbles her number down. I smile at her and stash her number in my pocket before apologizing again and heading out.

Making my way back home, I try to digest everything I've learned. Feeling like I've just opened a can of worms, I pause at the end of the drive to catch my breath. I feel weaker today. Not my body, but my mind. I've been distracted by Ryder and he hasn't even been here. Three days may not seem like a long time, but when your days are numbered, each one counts.

A black SUV is waiting in the driveway when I approach.

Ryder exits and stops when he sees me standing alone. Suddenly, all of the emotions I felt before my run came back and I feel like I'm going to be sick. He's still in his wedding attire and his hair is disheveled. He looks like he went on a three-day bender.

His presence brings relief, but jealousy is an unexpected co-pilot.

*What could you possibly be jealous of? His dead ex? The floozy he's been hooking up with at his club the past three days?*

Why can't I just hate Ryder so I can stop being distracted by his piercing eyes and the ink peaking out near his collar? I haven't learned anything about him to make me hate him, only that he was bred from evil. That should be enough, but right now it's not.

He married me and left me for three days, so no matter what I feel, or don't feel, I'm going to make it known that I'm not the kind of woman who puts up with this. Unfortunately for my new husband, I have a strict "get even" policy.

# Chapter 15

*Ryder*

D evina walks up the drive. Alone. Surely, she can't be so naive to believe she could leave on her own.

"Where were you?" I don't mean to yell, but she's still at the base of the drive.

Her stunned expression turns to anger and she marches to me, ignoring my question. "Where the hell were *you*?" She points at my chest with her dainty finger. I clench my jaw to keep from laughing at how adorable she is.

"Let's go inside and I'll explain everything. I thought Declan would have called you." I reach for her but she pulls away.

"Why would my brother have to update me on the where-abouts of my husband?" Placing her hands on her waist, she cocks a hip to the side. I should throw her over my shoulder and punish her for being such a brat, but I know I'm in the wrong here. At least, from her perspective.

"Devina, come inside and I will—" My plea falls on deaf ears as she pushes past me and makes her way up the stairs. I have no choice but to chase after her with my tail between my legs like the fucking puppy she's turned me into.

Once we're inside, I shut the door and turn to plead my case but she's already halfway up the stairs.

"You can't be serious, Devina." I follow her but she's deter-mined to get away from me. I should just let her take a time-out in her room, but I'm drawn to her in ways I can't explain.

"Unfortunately, I can't take you seriously, Mr. Totaro. You married me, danced with me, *kissed me*, and then left me without so much as a text. I haven't heard from you for three days and you're out doing god knows what, allegedly with my brother?"

*So she did think about the kiss. Hopefully, as much as I did.*

"Well if you'd let me explain, perhaps you would realize how ridiculous you are being," I snap at her, making her cheeks fume pink. I cut her off at the top of the stairs. Blocking her is easy with her being a fraction of my height. She crosses her arms and huffs.

"Declan and I got into a bit of a bind. An explosion, actually, and I was unconscious for a few days." The more I speak, the crazier I sound.

She cocks a brow and drops her arms. Her eyes spark with recognition. "The women. You were there with them?"

"Yes! I was with those women!" I raise my hands in a hallelujah but instantly regret the words as soon as I say them. "Wait, how do you know about that?"

"The news this morning. Twenty women were brought to a hospital and...are you telling me you saved them?" Her expression softens but I can tell she isn't letting this go completely. She's hurt, and rightfully so. This could have been avoided if her idiot brother had given her a call on my behalf—or if he hadn't given me a bomb to begin with.

"I swear, I got here as fast as I could." I retreat a step, knowing she's more receptive when I give her space. "I'm sorry Devina."

My gaze is drawn to her lip as she bites down and I want to pull her in to inform her that I'm the only one who will be doing that from now on. But I don't. I can tell she's at war with herself, but as soon as she notices I'm staring, one side wins, and it's not in my favor.

Her expression becomes firm once again. I wish I knew what she was thinking.

Am I allowed to kiss her? I'm her husband after all.

In a normal relationship, this would be the appropriate time for me to grovel and worship her until I gain her forgiveness. But this isn't a normal relationship. Still, I reach for her and pull her to me in an embrace. Her back stiffens and she freezes in my arms. "I'm sorry." Two words I'm not familiar with, but I'd say anything—do anything—to gain her forgiveness.

Just as she begins to melt into my arms, she shakes her head and pulls away. "I don't believe you."

I'm in shock when she walks past me and slams the door to the guest room.

The rage that was buried under guilt boils over and I see red. I don't know who she thinks she is, but no one slams a door on me. I've had a knife held to my throat, a gun held to my head, and most recently, a bomb blasting me into next Tuesday. But a door shut in my face? Not. Happening.

"Devina," I seethe, trying to contain the beast. "Open this door now."

"I don't think so," she sings from the other side.

"Open this door, Devina!" I yell back with a pound of my fist.

"Devina's not here right now," she echoes.

A frustrated sigh leaves me. This woman is impossible. I can't deal with this.

Fiona clears her throat behind me and I turn to face the second to last woman I want to be dealing with today.

"Make her come out of this room, Fiona," I command, pointing to the door.

"From what I've seen, you can't make that woman do anything she doesn't want to do, sir." She smirks and I roll my eyes.

"I'm going to get cleaned up. Watch this door. When it opens, I want to be told immediately."

She nods, but I have a feeling she's just as frustrated as my wife.

I see red until the warm water hits my back. I wasn't out running around for god's sake. I was recovering from injuries obtained while saving the lives of twenty girls. I didn't do it to be labeled a hero, but it's certainly a slap in the face that my wife has now labeled me the villain.

God, she's infuriating. Her pale cheeks were rosy with anger, her bright green eyes darkened with hate. Even her voice was laced with delicious venom as she tried to harden herself toward me. Then I remembered she mentioned our kiss. The kiss I haven't been able to forget. The kiss that ran through my mind right before the world turned dark.

I needed more of that, but it feels impossible now that she won't even open her damn door. Frustrated and rock-hard thinking about my beautifully vicious bride, I turn the water cold before stepping out and drying off.

Making my way through the room to the closet, I see my bed, which looks slept in. A satin nightgown lies discarded on the floor. *She was here.*

I pull on a pair of black sweats and a T-shirt and try to calm my racing thoughts before I get to Devina's door.

I knock.

No answer.

I knock harder.

No answer.

*Maybe she snuck out when I was in the shower.*

I lean my back against the door and slide down to the floor. "Devina. I need you to open this door. Please."

No answer. Leaning my head against the door reminds me of the bruise that is still sensitive to touch. "I'm truly sorry, little sparrow. I came back to you as soon as I could." I feel like an idiot. I could be talking to myself for all I know. "Okay. I forfeit. You win. But I don't know what to do now. What the hell do I have to do?"

"I don't know," a quiet voice responds. I can tell she is next to the door, mirroring me.

"If you would open the door, we could talk about this." I try my luck once more.

I hear her push against the door to stand and I scramble to my feet eager to lay eyes on her. Touch her. Fucking anything at this point.

A click solidifies my fate for the night when she turns the lock.

Not believing that she would turn me down again, I try the handle only to see that she did, in fact, lock the fucking door.

"I've tried to be nice, sparrow, but I'm not a patient man. I will ask one more time. Open this door or I will break it down." I fist my hands at my side waiting for a response.

Silence.

I believe the only thing I can do now is prove to my wife that I am a man of my word.

# Chapter 16

*Devina*

He's a liar. Most men are. I shouldn't be surprised.

I pick up my book and head back to my bed. I'm nearly settled in when the first bang strikes my door.

*So dramatic.* Like he's really going to—

Oh no.

He did.

He kicked my fucking door in!

Shards of wood scatter around his feet as the heavy door swings back and hits the wall. Our eyes meet across the room, both of us angry, neither of us willing to back down, until his gaze travels south and I realize I'm in a nightgown. I've been betrayed by a strappy satin fabric that does nothing to hide the scars I try so hard to forget.

Suddenly, my anger is replaced with shame and I reach for a pillow to shield myself.

"Get out of my room you caveman!" I yell, but he doesn't seem to hear me because he slowly walks toward me with his hands slightly raised. Like he's about to snatch up a rabid animal. Maybe I am one. Maybe I should attack and claw his fucking eyes out.

My vision blurs with tears and I toss my book at him, missing. The afternoon light does nothing to help hide me. I feel naked. Vulnerable. *Ugly.*

"Not what you expected, Mr. Totaro?" My words shoot daggers at him but he walks through them unphased. "Are you mad you got stuck with a defective model?" I strike again, but his steps only quicken until he is at my side reaching for the pillow I'm now clinging to.

I need his anger. I need something to snap me back. I close my eyes praying that when they open, this will all have been a bad dream. He's pulling the pillow that I refuse to let go of and before I know it, I'm falling off the bed.

He catches me right before we both crash to the floor. "Devina, look at me." His voice is calm and gentle.

I shake my head. "No. You need to leave now," I say through gritted teeth as I wrap my arms around my stomach and wait for him to go. As if that could hold back the tears that are now flowing freely against my will.

He pets my hair away from my face before bringing his gentle touch to my cheek, cupping my face in his hands. Tilting my face to his, he speaks in a low demanding voice, "Sparrow, look at me."

I force myself to look at him, prepared to see pity and disgust. Instead, I'm met with a heated, lustful gaze. We feel frozen in time. My desire to hate him is quickly being overpowered by a new desire to melt into the hands that are holding me with such care. I can see his reservation. The dark eyes that are peering into my soul are telling me he's calculating his next move, at war deciding what to do next.

His hands release me momentarily, but only to fall to my hips and pull me on his lap to straddle him. A hand moves up my back drawing me closer to him. A switch flips internally. I can feel it in him. He extinguishes whatever was holding him back and a dangerous smirk emerges. *That fucking smirk.*

"Fuck," he growls, and I know.

I know I can't hate him.

I've lost...but apparently, so has he.

His mouth crashes to mine and against my better judgment, because that version of me has taken a sick day, I wrap my arms around his neck and pull him closer.

He wraps his large arms around my thighs, his fingers digging into my skin, and I instinctively lock my ankles around his waist as he stands. We fit perfectly. A puzzle snapped together.

The heat from our kiss has traveled down to my core and I can feel it has the same effect on him. He turns to walk out of the room, and I break our kiss.

"Where are you taking me?" I manage to say as he sprinkles kisses along my neck.

"You're my wife. *My* little sparrow. This is your house and this"—he kicks a door open to walk inside—"is our room. *Your* room. When I make love to you for the first time, it'll be our bed." He kicks the door closed and walks me to the bed before gently placing me down on the satin covers.

I cringe as his fingers draw a line down my arms and his fingers gently caress the scar from my elbow to my wrist.

"Don't do that." His words are harsh, but his eyes never leave mine. "Don't ever do that, Devina."

"Do what?" I blink, breaking our connection and pushing myself further up the mattress to put space between us.

A fire ignites in him. He becomes a predator as he slowly follows me, crawling until his body hovers over mine and I'm captured between the weight of him and the strength of his arms that now rest on either side of my head.

"Don't hide yourself from me," he says through lips that are now hovering over mine. "You can hide yourself from the world, but when I said my vows, you became my world. A world I intend to explore until every inch has been discovered. Is that alright with you, my beautiful bird?"

I had no rebuttal. No one has ever made me feel wanted. Not that I dare give anyone the opportunity. He demands all of me, but I'm no longer my own to give. I've already been conquered by death but all I can think of when his hungry stare is seeping into my soul is that I choose to celebrate life.

"Y-yes."

# Chapter 17

*Ryder*

F ear radiated from her when she saw my gaze fall to her arm. *Fire. She is afraid of fire.* That's what she's been hiding all along. Like that could ever deter me. She can't see how beautiful she is, which makes me want to convince her even more.

I eagerly accept her invitation with a kiss. Her body shivers beneath me and I raise us both to pull her nightgown up and off her. I still feel like she wants to hide.

"You're beautiful." I appreciate her body, the body she's willing to share with me.

"I'm broken," she states, too confident with these words.

"Then break me, Devina. Break me so I can lie shattered and entwined in all of the pieces you won't let anyone else see." She lies back as I run my fingers down her chest and over her stomach.

I lean down and bite the inside of her thigh. Her back arches as she sucks in a hiss between her teeth. I mend the sting with my tongue. Her hands make their way to my hair and her fingers latch on, holding me between her legs as my lips graze hers, making her moan.

"I need you. Now, Ryde."

I give her one finger. She's tight as I flatten my tongue to her clit, my finger pressing up to the spot that will make her come undone. She tenses with a sharp breath in and I pause. I don't want to punish her, but she did make me kick down the fucking door.

"Please," she begs.

"What's our word, sparrow?"

"Fly," she whispers.

I reward her with another finger and she begins to meet me with the thrust of her hips. I lick her and nip at her lips before diving in, consuming her with my mouth. I can feel her clench around me as she comes undone on my hand.

Her chest rises rapidly as she rides out her climax. With lustful eyes, she watches as I suck one finger clean before offering her the other. She takes it eagerly, sucking hard enough to make my cock twitch.

"I can already tell you're going to be such a good girl," I growl, making a rush of heat flow between our entwined legs.

I line myself up with her, feeling her arousal dripping down her ass, soaking the sheet beneath her. She drags her nails down my back as I enter her, pushing myself to the hilt. Her gaze meets mine and the world stops. She. Is. It. She is everything I didn't know was missing.

"Ryder," she says impatiently. "I need you to fuck me."

It takes every ounce of me not to lose control at the sound of her words. What my wife wants, my wife gets.

# Chapter 18

*Devina*

The warmth of the morning sun wakes me. My body is sore in the most satisfying way. As pieces of last night begin to flood back, I'm filled with a different warmth. A foreign heat that is quickly followed by uncertainty and fear of this new emotion. He spent hours tracing every inch of me last night. The attraction that I now know is mutual, drowned out the world around us until there was only Ryder. Only me. Only us. I learned how easily I responded to his touch. He learned what brought me to whither beneath him and see stars.

I stretch and reach across the bed to find him, only to be greeted by a note on his pillow.

***I wouldn't have been able to get out of bed if I spent another minute in it with you. There's something I have to do. Be home soon. Love, Ryde***
*Love, Ryde.*

Is that what this is? This feeling that is simultaneously causing me to smile like an idiot and bringing on a wave of nausea? I should be happy, but I cringe at the realization that my entire situation has just become so much more complicated. He won't love me when I kill his father. He won't love me when he sees me wither away to nothing and the cancer slowly eats at my body. More importantly, I can't love him. Not in the way that someone deserves to be loved. I'll be gone soon and I have to finish what I've started.

I find my nightgown on the ground and make my way to the guest room to call Taylor from my burner. He answers on the first ring.

"Hey, stranger. How's married life treating you?" His sarcasm is not appreciated.

"Kicking my ass, Tay. Did you find any dirt? Anything that can help me?"

"Looks like the Cap holds a charity event each year. Ironic. I didn't know pure evil could be charitable. Anyway, I got hold of one of the invitations. Three weeks."

"Great, I can wait three weeks," I say out loud, but mostly to myself.

"What did you have in mind? I can get cameras in place. I have the information for all of the vendors and the location—one of his hotels."

"Honestly, I can't think straight at the moment. Give me a couple more days and we can catch up again. We have time." *No, we don't.* I'll never have enough time.

I stash my burner under the mattress and make my way back to the closet in our room. I've been living out of a suitcase for long enough and I'm sure Ryder has a T-shirt I can borrow until the rest of my things arrive. I walk in and the recessed lighting illuminates the space. I'm immediately welcomed with a handful of floor-length gowns in various shades of green. My first instinct is to be jealous that he still has Hannah's clothes in here, but once I check the tags I know they weren't meant for her. She was nearly six feet tall and slender. I'm not even five and a half feet after a good adjustment. *All of these are my size.*

"Ms. Totaro, will you take your breakfast in your room this morning?" I jump at Fiona's words.

"Jesus, Fiona, you can't just sneak up on me like that." My mind must be somewhere else if I didn't hear her approach.

"He asked me to get you out of that room, you know," she began. "I have taken care of this family for decades, but you had every right to be cross with him." She wagged her finger at me.

"Ha, I did, didn't I?" I laugh.

"He ordered all of this for you," she says with the tilt of her head in the most endearing way. "He can be a handful, but he has a good heart."

I don't know what to say, but I let myself smile knowing she's not lying. She takes my hand in hers to pat it before turning to leave.

"Hey Fiona," I run my fingers across the garments as I make my way toward her. She's seen me now, yet she seemed unperturbed by my mangled flesh.

"Does my arm not surprise you?" I ask.

"Oh no, sweetie. We all have scars, and I'd bet these are the mildest form of yours."

There is no sympathy, no pity. Just compassion. It would seem that in this house, I'm seen. I'm wanted. I'm accepted without fear of judgment. I nod silently. If I speak, I may just fall apart.

"I've brought you some toast, dear. Get dressed and come down to the kitchen. Your husband has left word that he will be home in thirty minutes." She stops and turns back at the door with a cocked brow. "I believe he is still trying to earn your forgiveness. Make sure he deserves it before you give it."

She's officially my favorite person.

After pulling my hair up in a ponytail, I take a quick shower and pull on the softest lounge set my body has ever felt. There are only a few with long sleeves, but it's nicer than anything I have ever owned. My family is wealthy, but Ryder seems to have a completely different level of wealth and it's apparent down to the labels on the clothes he's filled my closet with.

Making my way down the stairs and heading to the kitchen, I find Ryder casually leaning against the counter with a cup of coffee. He's in a black hoodie and joggers. He looks so different from the suit he wore at our wedding. It's been only days since that happened, but I'm realizing now that I haven't spent a whole lot of time with my dear husband.

"You're wearing long sleeves."

"You're observant," I reply, making my way toward the coffee pot.

"I thought we talked about this last night." He places his cup on the counter and folds his arms.

"We didn't do a whole lot of talking," I reply, looking over my shoulder. Is he going to be one of those husbands who has to control what I wear? The thought sickens me, but I know that if he is, I'll have to put up with it until I get the job done.

He makes his way to me but doesn't stop until his body gently, yet possessively presses into my back. Trying not to spill my coffee, I repress the urge to press back into him.

"What are you doing?" I ask, setting my mug down. "You're going to make me spill."

"I told you not to hide from me." His breath is warm against the shell of my ear.

"I'm not 'hiding' from anyone. I like to cover myself so creeps like you don't come on to me." Placing my mug on the counter, I turn to face him, poking his strong chest with my finger.

"Is that so?" He towers over me, the heat from his gaze slapping me right in the fucking clit.

"Is. that. so?" He asks again, amused by my attempt to dig my heels in.

"I wasn't fucking around, little sparrow." He grabs the bottom of my shirt and pulls it over my head, tossing it on the floor. "Aren't you going to ask me where I was this morning?"

"Do I need to know?" I'm standing in a kitchen. In a sports bra. The thought of anyone walking in makes me uneasy.

"I think you might want to know." He leans down and plants a gentle kiss on my lips. I'm not sure where we're going from here, but with thoughts from last night still swirling in my mind, I greedily accept the gesture.

"Well then, the anticipation is killing me. Where were you,

Mr. Totaro?"

He takes a step back. With an impish grin, he peels his hoodie off exposing his bare chest and...a wrapped left arm.

"What did you do?" The words are barely audible.

He begins peeling the clear wrapping away to expose black ink forming thick tree branches up to his elbow. He reaches for me, bringing my arm against his, and I see what he's done.

He now wears a mirrored image of my pain. The permanence is of a nature I can't possibly return. My eyes are wide with tears, I can't form words.

"You did this for me?" The weight in my stomach gets heavier. He has no idea how I received my scars. "Didn't that hurt? Your arm is...ruined." I should have forgiven him. I should have just been happy that he came home in one piece. But I didn't and now...now he looks like me, except the black ink is much more prominent than the faint pink scars on my arm.

"Don't you think it makes me look tough?" he asks with a low chuckle, but I can't see the humor in what he's done. I'm in awe, I'm speechless. "I know yours make you look like a damn warrior. You're not ruined, little sparrow. You're stronger than you'll ever know. I'm sure the pain I endured is minimal compared to how you received yours." He runs the palm of his hand over our arms, which for better or worse, now match forever.

"I don't know what to say," I finally relent.

"You can say 'You're the world's best husband, Ryder, and I'm going to reward you with my forgiveness'," he mocks. For a scary mafia man, he certainly has let down the facade with me.

"You're forgiven." I can't help but smile. Placing my hand on his naked chest, I graze my fingers over the ink that's been there before he met me. I wonder what story these lines are telling. "But don't you ever leave me like that again." An unfair demand, considering I'll soon be gone and forgotten.

"Never," he says before bringing his lips to mine, consuming every inch of my soul.

"Good, can I put my clothes back on now?" I ask.

"Not yet, I have one more thing for you."

# Chapter 19

*Ryder*

I can't tell if I've completely won her over, but my next move is sure to earn me some husband points. A ping of regret bounces around my chest as I let her go, but my new ink wasn't the only plan I had and I have to back away to deliver it.

"You hungry?" I ask, making my way back to the fridge.

"I could eat." The combination of her word choice and sultry voice ignited parts of me in a way I can't describe.

I pull out a brown paper bag and set it on the counter. Taking a seat, I watch as suspicion is painted on her face. She saunters over to the bag curiously.

"Leftovers?" she asks.

"Not quite. Take a look."

"I've watched too many 'what's in the box' videos. Tell me what it is." She crosses her arms but smiles.

I reach in to grab a clear box and she's relieved when she sees the top tier of our wedding cake. Miniature versions of us sit on top. I pluck two forks from the bag as she scoots onto the nearest stool.

"What do you say, Mrs. Totaro, shall we partake in a wedding tradition?" I ask, studying her reaction and offering her a fork.

"Aren't we supposed to eat this on our anniversary?" she challenges with an arched brow, the corner of her mouth pulls her lips into a sultry smirk.

"Well, I thought you might say that. But we didn't get to eat cake at our wedding, so we're no longer obligated to abide by that rule," I reassure her.

The sly smile on her face makes a dimple more evident and her gaze sparkles with impish intent. "Well, there's one tradition I was looking forward to."

I can read her mind. Dropping the forks, we lunge for the cake taking handfuls before not so elegantly trying to shove it in each other's faces. Cake flies across the kitchen. Frosting smears on our clothes and hair. I try to stand before she strikes again.

My height gives me an advantage, but she's clearly a competitive woman, not wavering in her attempt to smear me with frosting. We bob and weave as she squirms out of the chair to make a run for it.

"Oh no you don't!" I pounce, grabbing her around the waist with one arm as she squeals. She kicks her feet in the air as I effortlessly pull her back to the counter.

Fumbling over a stool, I try to cushion her impact as we crash to the ground. She's on top of me. Breaths heavy, she uses a finger to swipe frosting off of my cheek. I nearly come undone as she sticks her finger in her mouth and hollows her cheeks.

A blanket of silence covers us. She's a beautiful mess, and she's mine. Her hair has fallen out of her bun and I palm it away to bring her sweet, frosted lips to mine. A quiet moan leaves her and I know, I've truly been forgiven.

"Fiona isn't going to be happy about this." She sits up taking in the mess that we've made.

"Well, we better get out of here before she catches us then." I wink as we stand. "What about one more tradition?" I ask, lifting my bride to carry her upstairs and over the threshold of our suite.

With the shower running, I sturdy her before me. I unzip the front of her bra and run my fingers up and over her shoulders taking her in as the cloth falls to the floor. Her eyes are connected to mine as I kneel down, hooking my fingers at the waist of her pants, dragging them down until they pool at her feet and she steps out.

I kiss her stomach before pulling her leg up and over my shoulder giving me better access to trace her center with my tongue. She leans back to brace herself on the counter as I continue to nip and tease her before flattening my tongue, earning a moan of approval.

She runs her fingers through my hair and pulls my head back when it becomes too much, but silently asks for more.

I stand to remove the rest of my clothes before wrapping her in my arms and walking us into the shower. Placing her under the water, she closes her eyes, allowing me to clean her face.

Her beauty overwhelms me and I'm caught staring like a wolf about to devour its prey. We take turns washing each other. A sweet smile floats across her face. I know I need to think of a million new ways to bring that smile out.

I lean in, my mouth finding her ear. "Say it again, sparrow." She knows what I want.

"I forgive you." Her eyes hold mine tenderly.

Her unreadable default is crumbling, and I can feel that she wants this as much as I do. Lifting her to me, I line myself up to her entrance, and with one thrust, I'm seated fully inside her. Her nails dig into my shoulders as I push her against the wall. I give her a moment to stretch around me.

She provides me a nod of permission once she catches her breath but as much as I want to consume her, I want to savor this moment more. Labored breaths and running water are the only sounds around us as I slowly push myself in and out of her. She tilts her head back as her hands find my face. Her fingers tenderly trace my jaw as she accepts me.

Her walls begin to tighten around me and I pause for her to take the reins and work herself through her orgasm. Her moans echo throughout the room. The sight of her coming undone, knowing it's my cock that has her unraveling is enough to push me over the edge, but I'm determined to stay inside her as long as possible.

I push us off the wall and bring us to the water. Setting her down and spinning her away from me, I watch over her shoulder as the water cascades down her breasts.

She leans forward placing her hands on the wall, inviting me to take her—and I do. It's not long before she's ready to come again and I wrap my arms around her middle, drawing her to me as I follow.

# Chapter 20

*Devina*

The wind blew past me as Scarlet pushed me higher and higher. "Kick your feet!" she would yell after every push. The goal was to go so high you would fly over the top. Eight-year-old physics meant a hard enough push and enough desire equaled endless possibilities. When her arms would become worn and we both laughed enough to leave us gasping for breath, she would yell at me to jump. And I would. Being airborne for three seconds felt like an eternity. Like I was flying. Until I crashed to the ground.

We would come home scraped, bruised, and dirty. But the jump was always worth the crash.

The past two weeks have left me with a high from the flight as Ryder and I fall into a routine. We almost feel like a real married couple. I mean we *are* a real married couple. A real *arranged* married couple. He's just busy doing dangerous jobs around town in the middle of the night and I'm secretly still trying to kill his dad. But every couple has their own unique challenges.

*Right?*

He comes home every night, just as he promised. I don't cover my arms at home, like I promised. I still want to hate him, but hating him is the farthest thing from my mind when he's towering over me with his "fuck me" eyes. He's already memorized my body in a way I haven't even discovered. His touch ignites something deep within me that I never knew existed.

I spend my nights in our room. We eat breakfast together. He even goes jogging with me when he's home. We're living in a bubble and it's all beginning to feel normal. The problem is that we're anything but normal and the lines I initially created in my mind and heart are being blurred to the point that I question whether or not they truly ever existed.

*The problem* is that I'm in a constant war against myself over Ryder Totaro. He's told me stories of his family. His brothers are as close as Scarlet and I were. He's aware of many of the vile and torturous things his father is responsible for, but he intends to legitimize their businesses. When he told me, his honesty cracked the wall I'd spent so long building to shield myself from the world.

We have one more week until my first, and hopefully last attempt at taking out Cap. Taylor is keeping me up to date almost daily, but with Ryder attached to my side, it's nearly impossible for me to do anything myself to further the plan.

Luckily, I gave MaryClaire a call and today we're planning to grab coffee at her uncle's shop and stroll around town to find a dress for the charity dinner. You know, normal girly things. But when we're done, Taylor has a device to drop off to me for the big night.

"Are you sure you don't want me to go with you?" Ryder asks from the closet as he steps out and straightens his tie.

I've never seen a man so gorgeous. A well-balanced mix of masculinity and beauty.

"A girl's day isn't a girl's day if your husband tags along." I stretch, admiring him and secretly wanting to invite him back to bed. I'm fairly certain he can tell I'm becoming more and more smitten with him every day, even though I try my best to keep him at arm's length.

"Your *husband* is not a tag-along, little sparrow." He pretends to be insulted, but I don't know that there isn't anything this man wouldn't give me if I asked. Leaning over the side of the bed, he plants a kiss on my thigh. "Looks like we were a little too rough last night. Why didn't you use your safe word, sparrow?" He rubs his thumb over a large bruise on my skin.

I fist his tie to bring his lips to mine. "I guess the pleasure outweighed the pain." He would have no way of knowing that as my body is becoming weaker, and I'm starting to feel the effects in a real and tangible way.

"Well, no more of that, Devina." He only uses my name when he's serious. "I'm sorry I hurt you." He sits on the bed to pet my hair away from my face.

"You didn't, Ryde. I promise."

"A driver will bring you to the cafe and will be available to you and your friend for the rest of the day." He caresses me once more before standing to fetch his suit jacket from the closet. "I have a meeting with your brother and a few others. I will be home early this evening."

"Great, hopefully, I'll have a new dress to show you for the gala." I smile.

"I almost forgot." He pulls out his wallet and sifts through a few cards before holding one out to me.

"What's this?" I ask, hesitantly accepting.

"It's a Black Card," he says as if it were the most common thing in the world. "No limit." He gives me a wink, kisses the top of my head, and turns to leave, while I sit stunned. I'm wracked with guilt feeling like this man would give me anything in the world, while I secretly plan to take everything from him.

# Chapter 21

*Devina*

F ully caffeinated and having eaten too many donuts to be
trying on this dress, I stand in front of the mirror, taking
myself in. The past few weeks have made an impact on how
I view myself. Or perhaps I just completely trust that Ryder's
views of me are authentic and truthful. He likes me bare when
he can see all of me. At least, what I allow to be seen.

The black satin hugs me in all the right places and is a beautiful contrast to my copper hair. My favorite feature.

"Are you ever coming out of there?" MaryClaire calls from
the other side of the door. She hasn't seen me yet, but I have
already explained my insecurities. She didn't freak out or ask me
any invading questions, but you never know what someone's
reaction will be until you stand in front of them.

"Coming!" I reply and take a breath before stepping out into
the shop.

"Vi! You look amazing!" I may not have known MaryClaire
for more than a few hours, but she says what she means.

I'm embarrassed in the best way. "Do you think Ryder will
like it?" I ask.

"Are you kidding? I haven't met him, but I'm pretty sure he'll
be counting the minutes until he can get you home and rip it
off. You are *hot* girl!" She fans herself.

*So, this is what it feels like to have a friend.*

"Well, I think this is 'the one'. Which shoes do you think?" I
slip on a few for a test drive.

"Definitely the rhinestones. You will be the bell of the ball, girl."

"It's not really a ball. It's just a charity event." I shake my head.

"This is your first time, right? It's not just a charity event. Everyone who's anyone will be there. There are photographers and media. A-list celebrities swarm there for a photo and a chance to get recognized for their good deeds." She rolls her eyes as she pulls a shawl off the rack and walks it over to me when she notices me looking at cropped jackets. "Being married to Ryder practically makes you royalty. Royalty doesn't succumb to society's standards. You *are* the standard Devina. I agree with Ryder. Don't hide it." Standing behind me in front of the mirror, she drapes the sheer fabric over my shoulders and stands back to admire the ensemble. I do feel like a princess going to a ball.

"Have you ever attended?" I ask, slipping the shoes off and stepping back behind the curtain to change.

"No, but my boyfriend will be going. We just started dating so I don't expect an invitation." She shrugs.

"Oh, what does your boyfriend do?"

"Ivan does something with art. Trading, I think? He sets up auctions and runs them if they are here in the States." We finish checking out and MaryClaire gives me all the juicy details about her and Ivan's whirlwind romance.

"He sounds like a great guy. I'm glad you two found each other."

"We totally have to double date some time!" She jumps up and down at her bright idea. "I know Ryder is busy, but you need to make more friends. I'm sure living somewhere new is lonely if you don't know anyone."

"Well, I know you, so I think I'm good for now," I assure her. The last thing I want is to meet more people who will feel obligated to attend my funeral.

We pass a few more shops before I get a buzz from my burner phone and remember it's time to meet Taylor. Parting ways, I head toward a boutique. A message from Taylor comes through.

**Taylor: Turn left. Fitting room.**

I enter the shop and grab a shirt, heading toward the back. He's waiting near a rack, and it takes every ounce of me not to wrap my arms around him.

"Hey, sis. Married life seems to be treating you well. You're glowing," he teases.

I don't know how to tell him I'm slowly but surely falling for my husband. "It's not horrible," I admit.

"Well, here is the detonator." He slips me a keychain. A Hello Kitty keychain.

"Really? You couldn't have put it in something...less juvenile?" I scoff.

"Hey, you used to love Hello Kitty," he protests.

"Maybe when we were twelve." I roll my eyes imagining him walking around with this thing all day. His looks rival Ryders. Tall, ebony hair, and sinfully beautiful eyes. But I'm pretty sure he used to pee in our pool, so there was never an appeal to love him more than I would a brother.

"Press the nose to set, press the middle of the bow twice to see the boom." He smiles proudly. He should be proud. He's the smartest person I know. "Make sure you're not in the building when you set it off. My guy is going in tomorrow to set up a big blast. Lots of fire," he warns.

"That's exactly what I want," I assure him.

"I know, I just worry. I can't imagine losing you too. It's bad enough I had to lose you to that Italian mobster," he jokes.

"He isn't a mobster." I smack his shoulder. "Okay, maybe he is. But I'm telling you the truth. He isn't so bad. The apple fell far from that tree."

"Scarlet thought that Cap was perfect," he cautions me. "Just don't let your guard down."

"You know I won't." That's a lie.

"Look, I won't have my burner on me during the event. Just keep your phone on you and I'll call you as soon as possible."

Too much time has passed, and I know I have to get out of the boutique before my driver catches on that I'm not trying on clothes. He's moved the car block to block keeping an eye on me throughout the day, undoubtedly reporting back to Ryder. Or maybe not, but I can't be too sure.

I buy the shirt. The last thing I want to do is invite suspicion. Strolling out of the store, I find my driver parked near the entrance leaning against the SUV with a cigarette between his fingers.

"Hey, do you think I can have one of those?" I ask as he opens my door.

He chuckles. "I didn't take you as a smoker, Mrs. Totaro." He inhales but doesn't offer me one.

"I'm not, but is there a bad time to start?" I ask, tossing my bags into the back seat. You only live once, right?

"Your husband better not find out about this. You may think he's a big teddy bear, but he'll chop off my dick and staple it to my forehead if he finds out I've corrupted you." He eyes me cautiously.

"Well, it can be our little secret...I'm sorry, I didn't get your name. You've been more of the sullen silent type." I hold out my hand waiting.

"Sal," he grunts, retrieving a smoke from his jacket pocket and holding up a lighter as I place it between my lips. Mirroring his actions I suck, inhale, and slowly exhale. "Oh, look, she's a natural."

"Well Sal, how long have you worked with my husband? What kinds of things are you two doing when you're running him around town at all hours of the night?" He shifts on his feet. His broad shoulders and bald head remind me of the type of bouncer you'd see in an early 2000's rom-com nightclub. Although, I'm certain Sal could kill a man with his bare hands.

"You're a Sullivan, are you not? I'm sure Mr. Totaro's schedule is similar to that of your brothers."

"I'm not a Sullivan anymore." Suddenly the thought makes me melancholy. The girl destined to die too early has been given the gift of two different lives. Lucky me. "I wasn't privy to Declan's agenda. I only helped in one of his offices, filing paperwork. It was what he considered the safest position for me to be in."

"He's probably right. I have two younger sisters and I keep them far away from that part of my life." He drops his smoke on the ground before stomping on it and I do the same.

We ride home in silence and I allow thoughts of Ryder to consume me. He's done nothing but treat me the way a husband treats his wife. Looking back on the past two weeks, I recall the simple gestures of his hand on the small of my back as he passed me in the closet. He seeks every opportunity to touch me and I let him. When we sit down for dinner he asks me about my day, knowing mine isn't nearly as exciting as his. Before he leaves, he kisses my temple and I swear he inhales as if savoring my scent before leaving. Maybe, even if only temporarily, I could be a real wife to him.

How do you show your husband that you like him? I mean, 'like him' like him?

I've never been an addict, but pleasing him gave me the kind of high I now craved. He calls a sparrow. I should hate that. The plainest of birds, frail and meek. But when he calls me *his sparrow* I feel delicate, treasured, and cherished.

That's why I'm now in this confusing predicament.

I feel.

Most days I'm able to push the feeling down deep when he isn't with me. But today is different. Today I'm consumed with thoughts of him and they're drowning out any form of reason I've been clinging tightly to.

"Hey Sal, can we stop at the market on the way home?" I call up to the front.

"Sure, but I'm sure Fiona has the kitchen stocked." He peers back through the rearview mirror.

"Yes, but what kind of wife would I be if I didn't make my husband dinner now and then?"

They say the way to a man's heart is through his stomach, so I'd say this is an easy first step in testing the waters. An hour later we pull into the drive with a beautiful dress and bags of groceries. Sal offered me a stick of gum before he let me out of the car. Maybe today I made two friends.

# Chapter 22

*Ryder*

D riving home, I count the miles as they pass until I get to my little sparrow. She's consumed me, but I know any indication of this will spook her and she may very well fly away for good.

Each day I get a little closer. When our bodies are entwined, she lets her walls down, but only enough for me to peer over. Learning Devina has become my new obsession.

The way she sighs when retrieving a memory before she shares it with me causes an eagerness I'm not used to. I've learned bits and pieces about her childhood, which is always interesting. The way she speaks about Declan makes me sick to my stomach. She adores the man I hate, but I recognize that she wouldn't be mine right now if the cards hadn't fallen exactly as they have.

My initial idea of killing her barely made it to a cohesive thought before I realized I wanted nothing more than for her to want me as much as I want her. Hating her brother was still relatively easy. As the years have passed since Michaela's death, I've allowed hatred to drive me, motivating me into the position I'm in. I had every intention of using bullets to take down the Sullivans. What I haven't anticipated is a damn Sullivan becoming someone I'm growing increasingly needy for each day.

With every touch, every moan, every gaze she gives me before her eyes flutter shut each night, Devina has begun to heal pieces of me that she didn't break.

The sun is setting as I pull into the drive and park my bike at the bottom of the stairs. I can feel her before I see her as she opens the front door and leans against the frame.

"Took you long enough. I've been slaving away all day in this kitchen and you come strolling in whenever you tire of gallivanting around town." This has become part of our nightly ritual. I get home and she pretends to pester me about something. Tonight she seems to be a lonely housewife and is even wearing an apron.

"The unsavory parts of this town won't run themselves, my dear." I play my role in her little game as I make my way up the steps and sweep her off of her feet. "How will I ever make it up to you?" I kiss her neck, waiting to hear how delicious our makeup time will be.

"Nope. Not tonight. I really did make you dinner." She crinkles her nose and wiggles free from my arms.

I set her down and sturdy her before me. "You made me dinner?"

"Well yeah, that's what good wives do, right?" With her hands on her hips and her hair tied up in a bun, I'm not sure how seriously I can take her.

"Well, now I'm *really* happy to be home." I quip and take in a whiff of the aroma coming from the kitchen that has me wondering if she's trying to burn the house down. "What did you make? It smells like—"

Her eyes grow twice in size "Oh no!" She rushes off to the kitchen just in time to pull a burnt sheet pan out of the oven. "How did I manage to make an entire lasagna but burn a loaf of garlic bread?" She wipes her hair out of her face with the back of her mitted hand. She's adorable.

"I believe the bread is the most difficult part," I rationalize for her, though she isn't buying it.

"I'm sorry, I was trying to do something nice." She pouts as I lift her to sit on the counter.

"This *is* nice. But I'd be just as satisfied if you were the only thing on the menu tonight." I lean my forehead to hers. Her scent brings my desire to the surface. Lavender.

"I want to feel normal," she confesses.

"And you think lasagna is going to make you feel normal?" I pry.

"No, I think having dinner ready for my husband when he gets home will make me feel normal."

"Well, if it makes you feel better—"

She raises her hand to my mouth to silence me. "Fiona having dinner ready doesn't count."

"I don't think we were meant for that version of 'normal'. But I promise I prefer whatever we have happening right now." She tilts her head back with a sigh.

"Can we just forget this happened and find something else to do for the rest of the night?" She buries her face in her hands and I pause to take in the mess around the kitchen that I hadn't noticed until now.

The stench of burnt toast lingered and various pots lined the counters.

"I don't think I'll ever forget this." I chuckle, reaching into the sink and pulling up an ice cream scoop. My expression is asking a million questions.

She pushes me away and rolls her eyes. "Does it bother you that this isn't real?"

"Not real?" Now she has every bit of attention that wasn't already hers.

She wrings her hands together on her lap. "I mean, does it bother you that our marriage is a contract? An arrangement? We didn't meet in a café or at a park. Our first kiss was at our wedding. We haven't even been on a date." I sense that this has been bothering her.

"Every marriage is a contract. Besides, my parents were arranged." I drop the ice cream scoop back into the sink and find my way back to her. "Being completely honest, I don't care how I got lucky enough to have you here, in my kitchen, burning my dinner, but I'm glad that you are. If you had any doubt, you should know that I would happily choke down that charred loaf of bread if it meant I get to come home to you every night."

Her eyes widen as if realizing for the first time that this is more than a transaction to me. I lean down to meet her gaze. "This is not an arrangement, Devina. This marriage is real. It's real when I kiss you good morning. It's real when you come on my cock at night. And unless I've completely misread what has been happening between us the past few weeks, I believe every *fucking* ounce of this marriage is real."

"Oh." Her voice is barely a whisper as she shivers beneath my touch. I slide my fingers down her arm, just how she likes and her gaze becomes hazy at the sound of my confession.

She's right. This was an arrangement. A business deal between rival families. But it's been the best thing that has ever happened to me and fuck me for not making it abundantly clear to my wife.

# Chapter 23

*Devina*

*E*very ounce of this fucking marriage is real.

Stunned, I sit in silence. Why did his words feel like home? Scarlet was my home. I did this for her. But his words fill me in a way that nothing else ever did. I'm treasured, admired, and wanted.

I've spent years hiding myself. I'm a professional. Yet he seems to see past the most important parts of me that I want to keep in the shadows. His breath is so close, tangling with mine. My soul weeps for him.

"What can I do to make you believe me?" he pleads, a whisper.

I don't have an answer.

There is none.

A wrecking ball of desire knocks me off my feet. He's it. He. Is. Everything.

I want to deserve this. I want to deserve him.

Is this love? I wouldn't know. I only know spite, hate, self-loathing. I only know how to be broken. But the pieces of me desperately want to believe him.

He doesn't kiss me. He lingers just outside of my reach, but close enough to let the electricity sting me. Waiting. He wants to know I'm there with him. I know I am. I know I shouldn't be. I want to be.

I focus on his lips, biting mine, believing that if I can just keep them closed, keep them to myself, there will be no way for him to penetrate the fortress I've spent years building around my heart.

But it wouldn't be enough. Ryder would take my heart. I'd give it to him freely. He might shatter what is left of it, but I'll enjoy sitting in the aftermath of whatever is left scattered at my feet when this is all over.

Replying in silence, I meet him where he waits. My mouth brushing his is the permission he needs to consume me. All of me.

Breathing him in as my hands wrap around his neck, he deepens our kiss, and a low rumble builds in his chiseled chest. The sound alone is enough to make me moan into his mouth.

His arms circle my waist and pull me closer to the counter's edge. He hooks his fingers around my pants, and I obediently push up to allow him to pull them off.

He's on me immediately, pulling my shirt over my head and leaving me bare before him. His hands explore me as if it's the first time. As if I haven't noticed he's been memorizing me for days.

He kneels before me, taking my leg and peppering a trail of kisses up to my knee, nibbling my flesh the rest of the way to my core. He looks up at me with his devilish smirk. *That fucking smirk.* The one that melts me. His hand reaches to glide up my stomach and over my chest until I lean back on my elbows.

My head drops back in pleasure as he takes his time lapping up the wetness that appears at the slightest touch from him. He swirls his tongue as his hands grasp onto my thighs, holding me in place.

"So fucking wet for me, sparrow," he praises. "Always so fucking ready for me."

My body shakes as he draws my first orgasm, but his fingers are tight and unforgiving, holding me in place. I lie back, the coolness of the counter reminding me of where I am. What he's doing to me..

"That orgasm was *real*," he taunts as he stands and wraps my legs around his center.

He removes his tie and fastens it around me, removing my sight, but heightening every euphoric stroke of his skin against mine. I whimper in response, knowing he'll take his time punishing me for my doubt.

"My desire is *real*," he continues. I shiver in anticipation, hearing his zipper. He rubs his thick cock up and down my center with ease since he's made me gush all over the fucking cabinet. "Your reaction to me is *real*." He traces my nipples, and I feel them pebble beneath his touch. *Traitors.*

His hands find my wrists, pulling them down until I'm gripping the counter's edge. "You'll want to hold on, Devina. By the time I'm done, your pussy will always remember how *real* this is, just in case you ever think to doubt it again."

I brace myself as he enters me in one thrust, leaving me no time to adjust to his length. He pulls my legs until my ankles are perched on his shoulders, and his arm wraps around my thighs, drawing me to him.

"Say it, sparrow. Tell me you know this is real," he growls.

"It's real. We're real," I repeat immediately and loud enough to mute the thoughts still creeping in.

Releasing my legs, I instinctively wrap them around his center while his fingers find their way to my throat.

"I need to see you, Ryde," I plead. "I can't see."

"You don't need to see." He thrusts deeper if that's even possible. "You'll see when I want you to see." His grasp becomes tighter until I begin to see stars. "You'll breathe when I want you to breathe." He releases me, and the desire for air becomes secondary to the orgasm that is now threatening to throw me over the edge. "And you'll come when I want you to come." The pressure returns to my throat as he reaches for my clit with his other hand. "Because you're mine, and I'm yours, and...this. Is. Real."

We're launched off the cliff.

But I don't fall.

I'm flying.

# Chapter 24

*Devina*

F uck Ryder.

Fuck him for making me *feel*. I don't know what I feel, but feeling anything makes me feel everything and I've spent years trying to feel nothing.

His chiseled jaw that ticks when I challenge him. The way his new scar makes my heart flutter, knowing he got it just for me. His damn smirk, both mischievous and sexy as hell.

All the reasons I want to hate him.

All the reasons I'm beginning to love him.

I'm taking my coffee in the sunroom this morning, waiting for MaryClaire to come over. Having people in our home is something I'm still getting used to. While she's one hundred percent against going for a run with me, she's on board with settling in with our Kindles and reading books that make us kick our feet and giggle like teenagers.

My phone rings and I'm surprised when Declan's name flashes on the screen.

I kick my feet up on the chair across from me and take a large inhale before answering.

"To what do I owe the pleasure?" I hadn't spoken to him since our wedding. Not even after the 'three-day debacle'.

"I need you to get to the office to look over some paperwork with the attorneys."

"I'm doing great, thanks. Married life is blissful, although I'm sure my husband has told you. You see him more than you see me these days." My eyes roll to the ceiling.

"That's good news and I'm not exactly over the moon about having to spend time with your husband. For the record, we don't talk about anything but the job."

One thing I hate about myself is that I can't stay mad at Declan, even when he deserves it. "Fine. I can't come today. I have a friend coming over."

"Devina, this is time sensitive. Can't your friend visit you tomorrow?"

"No." *Jerk.* "I can be there in the morning. What is so time-sensitive that I need to drop everything?"

"I don't want to discuss it over the phone." His annoyed sigh makes me smile. I will always be *that* little sister.

"Well, I have a friend now, believe it or not, and she should be here any minute. I'll be there in the morning."

"Fine." He lets out a frustrated grunt before going silent. I know he wants to ask about any progress I've made but won't speak the words.

"Everything else is fine," I finally say.

"We'll talk more tomorrow."

He hangs up and I let my head fall to the back of the chair.

This was supposed to be a stress-free day of snacks and smut. Those are the best kind, right? Now, I'm mentally clenching a bat, swinging at the anxiety that's threatening to take over.

I've never had to question my loyalty. It has always been to Scarlet. To my family. But Ryder is my family now.

Fiona steps so softly that I don't notice her until she approaches the table. "Ms. MaryClaire is here for you."

My eyes remain shut as I chuckle. "Just MaryClaire, Fiona. Her name is *MaryClaire*. You don't have to be so formal," I tease.

She lifts her chin and gives me a wink as my husband strolls in with the paper to take a seat next to me. I wonder if Declan makes Darlene refer to him as 'Mr. Sullivan'. I never understood the formalities when you're all living in the same house, but to each their own, I guess.

"You're in my seat, Mr. T.," MaryClaire announces as she approaches the table, scooping up a danish and making her way to my side.

Ryder doesn't seem to take offense. He gives me a crooked smile and stands to place a gentle kiss on my forehead. "I should have known," he says. "I should be heading out anyway."

MaryClaire plops down in his place and our girl's day is officially underway.

I'm not sure what time it is when I wake up. After a few hours of reading, we decided to take a swim and MaryClaire headed home to her beloved, Ivan. One of these days I plan on meeting this mystery man.

I stretch and wiggle my toes. The oversized lounge chair is just as comfortable as our bed. The warm glow of the orange sky tells me it's late afternoon. Several days have passed without nightmares. In fact, I've slept better than I have in years.

This morning, I didn't think about killing myself and because of that, I realized how horrible it was that I had spent so many mornings plotting my demise when I should have been enjoying the limited time I have left. I woke in the embrace of a man. Before I could open my eyes, I was overcome with a heat that ignites and burns from the inside out. It's like coming home. I almost smiled and then I remembered Scarlet. She seems so far right now. I want to hate Ryder for it. My mind is so consumed with him that everything else becomes hazy in his presence.

Tomorrow we'll attend the gala. My one big chance to take Nico out. *The Cap.* Even his name screams entitled prick face. Who refers to themselves as...never mind. Not important. I need to check in with Taylor and make sure everything is set.

Grabbing my towel and Kindle, I head inside, stopping in the kitchen to grab a water bottle.

Ryder's house—*our house*—is much different than the estate Declan built for us. From the outside, it's a grand historic mansion of red brick and black shutters. The interior is sleek and modern, while still maintaining many of the original accents. The kitchen has bright white counters and warm oak cabinets. A white stone wall frames the stove, which has a special faucet for Fiona to fill her pots with water.

The family I come from had money long before I was born, but Declan, and my father before him, had maintained a humble home. I always assumed it was to not draw attention from unwanted eyes. But now, I think they just didn't care. Ryder has more money than God and he won't dare scrimp on a single thing, especially if it's something I ask for. Right now I don't have to ask for a lot and I'm grateful. It still makes me uncomfortable.

I wonder if it was a single moment in my childhood or a series of responses from the adults around me that makes me uncomfortable asking for things I need.

I lean against the counter of the island, the very one I was taken on not too long ago, and take a sip of my water. My cheeks flush at the memory. The slam of a door makes me jump and drop my water. The house is quiet once again. I grab the nearest towel to clean my mess when a blood-curdling scream sends a jolt of electricity up my spine, causing the hair on the back of my neck to stand.

This time, the noise doesn't stop.

Doing what you should never do, says every scary movie ever made, I start stepping toward the shrill screams. One foot is placed in front of the other until I'm standing at the top of the stairs that lead to the basement. This house is so old, it could be haunted. Right?

I want to turn around but my adrenaline is working overtime and I'm pretty sure I'm excited, not scared. Or at least, that's what I'm telling myself. The door is open, which must be a mistake. Ryder never leaves this door unlocked. It's the only place in the house I'm not supposed to go.

The lack of light at the base makes the stairs look like they descend into the deepest depths of hell. Complete black. The thought makes me shiver. My right foot lifts to begin my descent when I'm shocked back into the present with a large hand grasping my shoulder.

I shriek louder than the person screaming at the bottom of the stairs, only to turn and see Ronnie.

"You're not supposed to be here Mrs. Totaro." His voice is full of warning.

My eyes are wide with what I realize now is not excitement but indeed fear. I want to speak but I'm not sure what to say.

"Where is Ryde?" I need him here. He takes away the fear.

Ronnie's eyes shift to indicate that the gentle, loving, caring man I've started to fall for is at the bottom of those stairs, and he likely isn't the one screaming.

"Why don't you run along, Mrs. Totaro and I'll tell your husband you're waiting for him." He's going to tell Ryder I've been snooping around. But was I? Maybe they should have shut the door before they started torturing people.

Declan never brought work home. If he did, I never knew. I wonder if he has a secret torture chamber I'm not aware of.

I back away slowly before turning to run upstairs to our room. The screams grow faint with the distance of each step and disappear once Ronnie enters the door to the basement, closing and locking it behind him. *Soundproof.*

I wonder how many people have been brought to that room since I've been in this house. How many souls have been tortured, screaming in pain and fear?

When Ryder finds out I've lied, or realized who my target is, will I be taken down there? He doesn't love me, but he feels something for me. Will that disappear once he learns the truth? Will I live out my last days in a dungeon begging for death?

I find my way under the covers and curl into a ball. He's making me weak. Before Ryder, I would have done anything to make one particular man scream for mercy. Now, I wake up smiling and the darkness I've held onto for so long to keep me strong is slowly being lifted away.

I'm craving a man who makes people scream for mercy.

It's fucking terrifying.

# Chapter 25

### *Declan*

I stare out over the city as rain pelts against the conference room glass. Devina should be here any minute. It's too early to be drinking this scotch, but without sleep, yesterday has bled into today. I swirl the brown liquid in my mouth before letting it burn my throat on the way down.

Darlene knocks at the open door to announce my sister's arrival. As it turns out, her intelligence surpasses her intoxicating beauty and it was an easy decision to move her to an office position as a replacement for Devina after the wedding. She still manages the house but on a much smaller scale. I've asked her to find another house manager, but that process is still in the works.

"Thank you, Darling." I nod.

Devina steps past her with a smile and turns to me with arched brows. I know what she's thinking, but no, I'm not screwing my new assistant...or house manager...whatever she is.

She walks into my waiting embrace and I'm reminded of how fragile my little sister is. Despite that, there's a confidence about her that wasn't present before. As we take a seat at the long table, I realize she's wearing a sleeveless shirt. She notices me staring and clears her throat.

My eyes meet hers and I smile. A version of her that I haven't seen in years now sits before me.

"You wanted to see me," she states.

"Yes, I thought it would be more comfortable without the other suits in here with us." I spread out the forms in front of me and ready a pen. "By signing these, you receive thirty-five percent of each of the companies. Father set this up when we were little. You were to receive this once you were married. Because Scarlet is gone, I've arranged for you to receive the total of both of your shares."

Her eyes become wide, yet curious. "I don't know anything about running a company, let alone..." She scans the documents in front of her. "Nine companies?"

"You don't have to do anything beyond use your signature. If any additional pages require it from time to time, I will have a runner deliver them to you."

She reaches for the pen I'm holding out but stops. "Who are the other owners?"

"Myself and Ryder. That was the deal we made. If something happens to Ryder, you acquire his shares. If something happens to you, well, you get the picture."

"Why won't you receive them if something happens to me?" she asks.

"Because father intended to pick your husband and wanted it this way. He wasn't able to do that, but that doesn't change the stipulations in his will."

"So if I die, Ryder becomes a majority shareholder."

"That's right."

"And our family legacy falls into his hands. His family's hands."

"Correct."

"Does he know about this?" She taps the end of the pen against the desk, distracting me.

"He doesn't, but even if he did, I don't think he'd do something stupid to take it from you. He and I will be running these together now regardless of your ownership. But I'd still appreciate it if you would take care of yourself and not die before I have the opportunity to show him we can be a good team together."

She rolls her eyes. "Oh good, I don't have to worry about him staging my death to take over. Not that I ever did. I think he's growing fond of having me for a wife." Her cheeks flush and I look away, not wanting to imagine his hands on my baby sister.

"I have no doubt."

"So I just sign, and then what?"

"And then you're even more rich than when you walked into this office. You'll always be taken care of. Even if your husband wakes up one morning and decides he isn't so fond of you."

Her smile falters. I haven't been the best brother over the years, but I'll always make it a priority to care for her and keep her safe.

She grips the pen and takes her time sifting through the pages to plant her signature.

"All done." She caps the pen and places it softly on the table before leaning back in her chair.

I don't want her to go. I want to tell her that I miss her pushing my buttons and being in my space. I want to tell her to stay and have lunch with me. But she has a new life now and I have...well, I have businesses to run and a new assistant I'm still training.

We aren't the kind of people who share thoughts, hopes, and dreams. We're the people who sweep things under the rug and keep our secrets guarded at all costs.

I stand, causing her to follow my lead.

"I hope he truly is being good to you."

A soft smile spreads across her lips. She's known that our lifestyle is dark and dangerous and sickening at times. I've done my best to shield her from it and Ryder has given his word that he'll do the same. But I still worry.

"He's not what I expected," she says. "But in the best way."

Her eyes sparkle and I'm instantly relieved that she seems happy. It's all I've ever wanted for her.

She closes the distance between us and brings her hand up to the side of my face scratching the stubble that's become prominent after two days of not shaving. She used to do that when she was little. "I'll leave you to it then." She pats my face. "I want you to be happy too, Declan. Your *Darling* might be just what you've needed all this time."

With a wink, she turns on her heel to leave.

I can feel the heat rising in my cheeks and hope Darlene didn't hear the comment.

Little sisters.

They always know which button to push.

# Chapter 26

*Ryder*

"Where are they meeting?" I ask the man tied to a chair before me. He's been crying for an hour and already pissed himself out of fear. Not so different from the two men before him over the past few days.

"I swear, I'm just a runner. I don't know anything," he pleads. As if pleading for his life is magically going to make me spare it. He should know that his life was over the second my men picked him up off the street in broad daylight, not a single fuck given. "Please, I have a family. My wife. My wife—"

A blow to the nose shuts him up. I've allowed my own wife to soften me. Only weeks ago, I would have stuck a drill to his elbow until I got the information I needed. Now, I'll settle for fear and minimal blood. We do have an event to attend tonight, after all.

Blood splatters against the wall from the blow and the thick liquid pours freely from his nose. He doesn't attempt to blow his nose clean. People in our world know all too well that blowing a broken nose will lead to more swelling. And I'm pretty sure the majority of us have had our nose broken a time or two.

"Your boss. What's his name?" I growl. I'm growing tired of this game but there are still a handful of details I need to know.

"I don't know his name," he whimpers. "They call him 'IT'."

Ronnie enters the room, taking a seat by the door and stretches his arms over his head. This is a fucking game for him. Broken bones make his smile light up like fireworks on the Fourth of July. He's sick and twisted. Even more so than me, but that's why he's the best at what he does.

"Unfortunately for you, I'm out of time and you'll be getting to know my friend here. You could have saved yourself a lot of pain." I wipe my hands on a rag and toss it to Ronnie before leaning back against the wall.

Ronnie stands and swipes a hammer off the table on his way to me. "You should get upstairs. The Mrs. will be ready soon. You're going to need to clean up before you go." His eyes land on splattered blood, now staining my crisp white button-down.

"I need to know who IT is. I need to know where they're meeting next." The man in the chair stares up at me with hopeful eyes. Pathetic. "And find another place for us to conduct business. I don't want these pathetic fucks this close to my wife."

She was visibly shaken after a close encounter the other day with Ronnie, who left the fucking door open when he ran upstairs to retrieve something from my office—a mistake he won't be making again. I heard this from him, of course. When I asked her if she wanted to talk about it, she simply said she didn't and rebuilt the walls around her that I've been trying desperately to knock down. She thinks I didn't notice, but I notice everything she does.

He nods before turning back to the restrained man. I leave as his screams threaten to chase me through the halls on my way out of the door.

The basement is soundproof. No one hears the blood curtling bellows of the shit-bag men that end up here. But I can't chance this part of my life bleeding into the one I'm creating with Devina.

She has insisted on having full control of our room so she can get ready without interruption, so I make my way to the guest room to shower.

She's becoming more relaxed in our new routine. Our kitchen encounter must have left as much of an impact as intended, though she hasn't attempted to make dinner again. Thank God. I'd do a lot for that woman, but I'm not a glutton for punishment.

My fingers trace her skin every morning. On the days I am home, I run with her. I hate running. I feel like I'm always running toward her, but she's always running from something. *From me.* Every night we find peace in each other's embrace. I've memorized the simple touches that make her melt. The ones that earn me a brick from her wall. The ones that make her shiver and come undone.

*This is what I wanted.*

My phone pings on the nightstand. A note from Ronnie: **It's done.**

Good. One less thing I have to worry about. God forbid my wife stumbles across a dead man in the basement. I toss my phone back to the nightstand, knocking down the stack of books Devina left.

My wife and her fucking books. Her life is a damn romance novel. But she also gets whatever she wants, so I don't mention them. The sound of her and MaryClaire giggling like school girls will make the darkest of hearts smile.

Reaching between the bed and nightstand, my sleeve gets caught on something between the mattress. My mind tries to compute what I'm holding in my hand. A phone. This is not my phone. This is someone else's fucking phone.

Why is my wife hiding a phone in the guest room? I open it to find one name: Taylor.

Red. Everything is red.

My mind reels as I pace the room. Is this what she's been hiding? Taylor could very well be a woman. Right? Has she been spying for her brother?

I don't know what to think, but I know I need answers. I deserve answers.

I want to kick another door down on my way to her, but I rein in my fury and turn the knob painfully slow.

"Ryde, is that you?" she says from the closet. I take my time to walk over to the sofa and sit, my elbows on my knees, the phone burning between my palms.

Still considering how to approach the subject, I'm interrupted by my wife's presence as she strides into the room wearing the most exquisite satin dress and a pair of strappy heels hanging from her fingers. I almost forgot what brought me here. But her gaze, full of adoration and joy, quickly falls when her eyes land on the brick I'm holding.

Her face pales and I know. I know that whatever she's about to tell me isn't going to be something I want to hear.

"Don't ask me where I got this," I begin. "Who. The. Fuck. Is. *Taylor.*"

She composes herself, taking slow steps toward me, holding her hand out in a gesture for me to hand it over. I stand towering over her, but she doesn't indicate that she's afraid of me.

My usual tactic is to intimidate my enemies, but my petite wife would be having none of that. She pokes my chest with her finger, unwavering. "If you want to know, you need to give it to me."

Reluctantly I comply. She opens it, taps the name, and places it on speaker. Our eyes never break away. It's a battle of wills.

*Ring.*

I want to ring her neck.

*Ring.*

I should have ruined her and sent her back broken. More broken than she came to me.

"Hey, sis. I thought you were calling me tomorrow. Are you okay?" The man answers.

"Tay, my husband seems to have found the phone you gave me. Say 'hi'." Her posture shifts. One hand on her hip as she thrusts the phone up to my face.

And just like that, Devina has made me feel like a complete jackass again.

"Hey, too soon to call you brother?" He laughs in a deep voice. He fucking laughs. "Vi, I think it's about time you clue him in. I have to go. I'm sure you both have a lot to talk about right now."

He hangs up, leaving me speechless. Speechless, but still fuming.

"I think you need to sit down for this," she says, taking a seat on the bed, waiting for me.

# Chapter 27

*Devina*

Fucking Taylor.

Of course, we knew this could happen. I was careless. But we know what parts of our plan can be shared and what can't. So now is the time to come clean. Well, as clean as I can be with Ryder.

"It happened seven years ago..."

I tell him about the fire. I tell him what happened before the flames. I tell him that my Scarlet was taken and replaced with this hideous scar. I tell him who Taylor is, and who his mother was. I tell him of the life that never came to be.

I don't cry. I've cried enough. But it still pains me to speak the words out loud. He sits silently as I speak. I expect rage. I brace myself for the fallout.

When my story concludes, he takes a moment to digest what I just threw on him. Too long of a moment. The silence punishes me. I have to break it before it breaks me.

"I know what you thought when you saw his name on the phone. I can promise you that Taylor has been nothing but a brother to me, even more than Declan." I reach for his hand but he pulls away. Our room that has become our sanctuary is now tainted as my pain splatters along the walls.

"You don't know what you thought." He rubs his hands over his face with a sigh. "I mean, it's one of the things that crossed my mind, but I thought..."

"What?" *What could be worse than that?*

"I thought you were spying." He pinches between his brows and stands, beginning to pace back and forth. Of course, he knew deep down that I wasn't seeing someone else. I did marry him voluntarily.

"A *spy*?" I can't help but laugh. "You've got to be kidding Ryder. What would I possibly communicate back to the home base? That you are now fluent in how to bring me to climax?"

His face reddens and he turns to me with a halt. I should learn to keep my mouth shut, but then again, that's what got me into this mess. "I knew you were hiding something from me. Is this it? What else are you not telling me?" he demands.

"This is everything." Lie. I lied.

*I'm dying.*

*I'm in love with you.*

*I can't breathe without you.*

"And you're still looking for him. This 'invisible man'." He lets the words hover around us as if he's still pondering what to make of this.

"Yes." Another lie. Kind of.

It pains me how easily they roll off my tongue and how confidently I display them.

His face visibly softens as he tilts his face up to the ceiling letting out a frustrated grunt.

*Yeah, I feel that, my guy.*

"He's still out there." He approaches me quickly, reaching for my arm. Instinctively, I jerk away causing him to slightly raise his hands in retreat.

My shoulders relax and I allow him to take my hand. He traces my scars with a light touch. His scarred arm, mirroring mine. Now he knows how it came to be. I wait to see the regret on his face, but if it's there, he is keeping it hidden. I can't be mad. I've been keeping it all from him.

Right now, I would honestly give it all up to earn his forgiveness. To be everything to him again. Suddenly the fear of losing him outweighs the hate I've been nurturing, causing a sickening confusion deep in me.

"I'm going to find him, sparrow." A vow as sincere as the ones that bound us in this life. "When I do, he'll pay with blood."

"You don't owe me that." He doesn't. I lied. *I'm lying.* I don't deserve what he's so blindly giving.

"Maybe I don't," he reasons as he brushes my hair over my shoulder. "But because of *him*, there's a part of you I'll never know. There's a part of you that you're keeping from me. I can feel it."

I shake my head. I know now that I've let him get too close. Tears threaten to fall. My world spins. I bite my cheek to keep the words from spilling the name I don't dare say. He wouldn't think this way if he knew.

He can never know.

"You are, Devina. I can feel you. I know you. I was made for you." He braces my shoulders to keep me from swaying.

"I don't want to talk about this anymore." I can't look at him. He knows. He knows the worst parts of the night that broke me.

"We don't have to." He pulls me to him, embracing me in the arms that would likely snap me in two if he knew the truth.

"We don't? You're just forgiving me? Just like that?"

He gestures for me to sit while he takes the heels from me that I've been nervously holding. Kneeling down, he grabs my left foot, slipping the heel on before resting it flat on his chest to clasp it tight. My heart flutters at the gesture.

"You're mine, sparrow. I'll always protect what's mine." He places my foot back on the floor before reaching for the other and repeating the task. "I don't know what else I have to do to convince you of this." His jaw tenses but he places a kiss on my ankle before releasing me. "As for forgiveness, we'll handle your punishment later."

He stands and offers his hand to me. I squeeze my legs together, knowing I'll probably enjoy it as much as I hate it.

He doesn't have to convince me that he'll protect me. I just have to allow myself to believe I'm worthy of it. I want to be his. I want to savor the delicious words he continues to serve me, no matter how undeserving I am.

Taking his hand, I'm overwhelmed with guilt knowing that without a doubt, both of our hearts are destined to break.

One day soon, I'll be gone and none of this will matter. When he finds out and hates me, none of this will be important.

But his words make me feel like I'm worthy.

I don't deserve it.

I don't deserve him.

But I'm selfish enough to keep him.

The mission is now more complicated. I let him kiss me and my lips linger on his. After tonight, everything will change. Even if he doesn't know why.

# Chapter 28

*Ryder*

Devina's eyes sparkle as she looks out the window when we pull up to the casino. I step out first and round the car to take her hand to lead her inside.

She recovered from our misunderstanding quickly, making a joke about how funny I look when I'm mad and my nostrils flare. Nothing riles her. She didn't cower when I accused her. She owned it. She relived one of her darkest moments to make me understand, but I still don't know why she didn't tell me to begin with.

Perhaps she still doesn't trust me.

Perhaps I trusted her too much, too quickly.

I may have been inside of her more nights than not, but we're still strangers. Every time I feel like I'm making progress, she shuts me out. But tonight was different. She knew this might happen. She was prepared to share this with me, but I could tell she didn't want to. That bothers me most.

The cameras flash as we make our way inside. Our first public event as a couple. No one would know that not too long ago, we were having an earth-shattering marriage moment. Devina's eyes glisten as she looks up at me adoringly. A gaze that rivals her defiance, and sends the same shiver down my back.

I could sense her pulling further away when she was telling me something that was supposed to be bringing us closer together. She's guarded. Still. It's driving me insane. She's driving me insane. But tonight, I'll let it go. Tonight I'll enjoy my wife.

Cap certainly went all out for the evening. Many of the attendees from our wedding are here and scattered around the grand ballroom. We check our coats at the main door and make our way to the bar.

I take two glasses of champagne and hand one to Devina. She smiles and takes in the room.

"Ryder, great to see you." Philippe approaches. "Devina, pleasure."

He takes her hand in his and lifts it to his lips. If he wasn't my younger brother, I'd have something to say about how long he stares at her.

"Hello Philippe," she replies. Her rosy cheeks give her away. I know she's thinking about the day she thought she was marrying him.

"Hey Ryde, I need to catch you up on some things when you have a second."

"Sure, let me get Devina to our seats and I'll come find you."

I lead Devina to a table and pull out her chair. We're greeted by a server who delivers two more flutes of champagne.

"Tell me to stay and I will." I crouch down to her level, trying to read her.

"Ryde, we're fine. I promise." Her doe eyes don't fool me anymore. Devina is much too skilled at keeping her emotions in check, but there are things I have to take care of.

Couples pass by and stare at my wife. I know the men want her and the women envy her. I'm not the only one who notices. Her fingers instinctively float to her wrist to pull down a sleeve that isn't there.

This is the first time she has shown her body to the world since the fire. The body that has only been available for my eyes. I stand to shake off my tuxedo coat and drape it over her shoulders.

"I'm not cold, Ryder." She has to fucking push me about everything. She shakes off the jacket to hang it over the back of her chair.

"I didn't ask if you were cold, sparrow," I say as I unbutton my sleeves to roll them to my elbows displaying our matching scars.

She rolls her eyes, but I can see the shift in her demeanor.

She's happy.

I did that.

"Five minutes, okay?" I ask once more before kissing her head and heading over to my brothers.

Passing by the bar I see an unfamiliar face. A man with bright blonde hair and ice-blue eyes is staring at my wife. A woman approaches him and breaks his gaze. *Probably nothing.* But I feel like I've seen him before.

Luca and Philippe are in the hall.

"We have some news on the Bratva." Philippe gets right to business. "There seems to be a warehouse where they're keeping their merchandise. The problem is that everything is brought in large crates, and we can't get eyes inside to confirm what it is."

"First women, now this? What else do they have their fucking hands in?" Luca complains. I don't blame him.

We have enough to do and don't need the additional stress of cleaning up after Declan. He should be more than capable, but I suddenly sympathize with him after hearing Devina's story straight from her beautiful lips. "I'll get in touch with Declan and we'll go in solo to see what's going on."

"Just be careful," he says and links a map to my phone. "You'll have to park a block or two away. They have spotters out at all times."

"Yep, got it." I slip my phone back in my pocket.

"So, how's married life, brother?" Luca pats me on the back.

"Better than I thought," I reply honestly, although I'm not sure what I anticipated it to be.

"That so? So, are you saying you aren't going through with the plan?"

# Chapter 29

*Devina*

⊪|⊪|⊪ Wicked Game — Lusaint ⊪|⊪|⊪

A hand lands on my shoulder making me jump.

"Good evening, Devina. How rude of my son to leave you alone." Cap takes an uninvited seat next to me.

"He's looking for his brothers. Shop talk, I guess." My blood is boiling under my skin.

"Well, I'm glad I get a moment with you alone. I wanted you to know that I was very pleased with the arrangement your family made with us. My son seems to be happy and I'd do anything for my children."

*Scarlet was having one of your children.* I bite my teeth together to keep the words from slipping out.

"If there's anything that you need, I hope you know you can always ask," he says, gliding the back of his fingers up my exposed scar.

I stand abruptly, disgusted by his forwardness. I look around the room trying to maintain my composure.

"Thank you, Cap. I think I'd better go find Ryder. Have a nice evening."

My knuckles turn white from clasping my clutch as I bolt from the table. Taylor's key chain sits safely inside but I'm not ready to pull the trigger. I didn't think I could hate that man more than I already did, but there appears to be no limit to how grotesque he can be.

I pick up another glass of champagne from a passing waiter and make my way to the hall behind the bar where I last saw

Ryder.

The sound of hushed voices makes me stop.

"How's married life, brother?"

"Better than I thought," Ryder replies, and I can't help but smile. Maybe in another world, we would have had a happily ever after. But in this one, maybe we can settle for a happy until it's over. I take a step to round the corner and stop.

"That so? So, are you saying you aren't going through with the plan?"

"Look, I think that needs to be revisited at another time. She isn't who I thought she'd be."

Now I'm intrigued. I can feel my body heat and my breath get caught in my throat.

"She got to you. You're going soft," Luca accuses with an airy laugh.

"I knew you weren't going to break her." Philippe chuckles. "Well, as much as I would have liked to see Declan torn down when his baby sister is delivered in a broken pile of rubble and his company gone, I'm glad you took my advice. Who knows man, maybe it's all for the best."

Luca's eyes shift past Ryder causing him to turn and see me. I can't hide the shock from betrayal.

"Dev—" He takes a step toward me but I back away and turn to leave.

God, I'm so stupid. Of course, Ryder wanted to hurt Declan. I don't know why he wants to hurt him but at least I know now why he agreed to this arrangement. He doesn't want me for an alliance. He wants me for leverage. He wants to hurt my brother. *He wants to hurt me.*

I try to make my way to the closest side door but I know he's on my heels. Stepping out into the dark alley, I let the cool night air shoot through my lungs as I inhale deeply. The door slams behind me, but I know I'm not alone. His hand pulls me back by the arm until I'm pushed against the door that was supposed to lead me to freedom.

"Sparrow, look at me." *I can't.* "Jesus, Devina. Please look at me." The desperation in his voice sends a crack through my heart.

I meet his stare with fire, and I wish it would burn him. "I have nothing to say to you. I feel so stupid right now. You said this was *real,* Ryder, but it looks like I wasn't the only one keeping secrets." My voice cracks.

"Please let me take you home and I can explain everything. It's not what you think. What you heard probably sounds really fucking bad."

I reach to pull down my sleeve but realize I'm not wearing any.

I feel used, exposed, so vulnerable. He can sense my urge and draws his fingers up my scarred arm. I try to pull away but his chest is pushing into mine. I can't keep the tears from falling.

"Please," I beg. "Just let me go."

"Devina." His voice is grave as fingers find my chin and force my face back to his. "I can't let you go. I'll never let you go."

"Why not?" I breathe out.

"How can I let you go when you consume my every thought?" He speaks in a low voice making the hair on the back of my neck stand at attention. "You infuriate me. You make me want to fucking scream and for some reason, you can't see yourself the way that I see you, which drives me insane."

"And how is it that you see me?" I'm genuinely curious now.

"You're perfection, sparrow. You're worthy. You captivate me." My heart wants to believe him, but my mind refuses. "I'm so fucking in love with you, can't you see that?" His eyes shift back and forth searching mine. "And you love me too."

I try to swallow the lump in my throat. No way am I going to admit that. Not now, not ever. If I never say the words out loud, I can believe that it's not true.

I get a second wind and let out a weak laugh. "Love me! *Love me?* You don't even like me. You wanted to use me! And then what? Send me back to Declan? Kill me? I'm nothing to you, Ryder."

"Dammit Devina." I jump when his hand slams against the

wall beside my head. "You misheard me. I love you. I love *you*."

His lips devour mine in a possessive kiss and I hate myself for reciprocating. Every part of my mind is screaming for me to run and never look back. But the heat in my core is pulling me closer to him. I've never felt more at war with myself, because as much as I hate Ryder right now, I melt so effortlessly into him.

His hand releases my face only to wrap around me, pulling me impossibly close. Even in heels, I can only reach the back of his neck as he leans over me, but my fingers latch on just as enthusiastically as his do. Fire blazes between us and I'm not sure if it's love or hate fueling us.

This is the type of fire that burns deep, and I know I can't come out the other side unscathed.

He breaks away, my chest heaving against his, and his eyes search mine for forgiveness. I can't let him know he'll always receive that from me.

Instead, I demand, "Prove it."

As we make our way out of the elevator to the garage, my fingers brush his and he smiles to himself, taking my hand in his, swiping his thumb across my knuckles. *Fuck, make me swoon why don't you.* I'm still mad. How can I ever trust him again? But as mad as I am, he does something to me that I can't explain.

He's a fucking drug to me. Poison. With every kiss I need him more, the high something I've never tasted before.

Sal and Ronnie trail behind us as we make our way to the cars when a shot rings through the parking garage.

In one swift movement, Ryder pushes me back and releases my hand, using his other to grab the gun at his back. He aims and squeezes the trigger without hesitation.

I crouch with my knees to my chest, too scared to peek around the tires of the jeep that is keeping me very much alive at the moment. How does he know where to shoot? I didn't see a soul in that garage with us.

# Chapter 30

*Ryder*

I knew something was going on when I saw that Russian at the bar. I heard Sal instruct backup over the mic he wears so I know it's only a matter of minutes before they arrive. We only have to keep them at bay for that long. Unfortunately, I only have three bullets left and the other exit is on the other side of the fire.

There are stairs to our right and if we move fast, I can get her to the level below where our men are likely coming from.

"Devina— " I shout trying to make my way back to her. "We have to go. Now!"

I look behind me to make sure she can hear. She's crouched low with her hands over her ears but I see her reluctantly begin to move. She turns, locking eyes with me. Her gaze is full of determination and hope.

I know she trusts me to get her out of here. She's on her feet reaching for me when her eyes shift and mine follow her line of sight. A bullet strikes Sal through the neck and sparks fly on the pipes above us as the bullets ricochet. Her arms wrap around me and we twist as I'm thrown back to the cement. Her face contorts and she pinches her eyes shut as I cradle her and we fall to the ground. Her body falls slack on top of mine with a burst of heat running over my hands.

Anger rushes to the front of my mind, knowing I don't have enough bullets to kill the people who are reigning fire down on us.

I roll us over so I can inspect the damage. She's been hit in the back. It didn't go through or it would have hit me. *Fuck Devina, why did you do this?*

The doors open and backup begins to flood in, shooting past me. Two guards fall to their knees to reload while Ronnie grabs me at the waist to pull me back toward the stairs.

"I can't leave her!" I fight my way back but they're stronger than me, which is why I hired them. Of course, this seems to present quite a predicament because I'm not leaving my wife in the middle of a war.

"I can't get you both Ryder," Ronnie yells. "She's down. Let me get you first and we will get her."

I elbow at his face, stunning him enough to release me as I run toward Devina, throwing myself back over her body.

# Chapter 31

*Devina*

S al is gone. He was shot through the neck. A sharp pain makes its way through my body before I begin to feel numb. I'm falling but I know I've been hit. The taste of copper floods my mouth as I cough.

I can barely open my eyes.

I can't feel my fingers.

I must be in shock.

I can't breathe.

Better me than him. I was already dying anyway.

There's something heavy on my chest, on my stomach, on my legs. I'm not sure what hurts worse, the jarring shock ringing throughout my body, or the realization that he'll never know that I love him.

# Chapter 32

*Ryder*

Her breath is shallow but warm against my cheek. I squeeze her, nuzzling my face into the crook of her neck. I know I must be crushing her, but I need to cover as much of her as possible. I have survived worse than a few bullets, but I won't survive if she isn't here.

Ronnie takes out the last gunman and orders our remaining men to scan the area.

I push myself up onto my elbows so I can brush the hair away from her face.

"Devina, I'm here. Can you hear me? Baby, please open your eyes. Don't leave me. Don't you dare leave me!" I plead.

Her black dress is dirty from the ground and darkening as crimson smears across her middle.

She's been struck just below her ribs. Blood is coming as though a floodgate has been opened. I pull her toward me, putting pressure on her wounds. Seeing her blood on my hands unleashes something feral deep within me and the need to kill overpowers my thoughts.

I know they're all dead but they didn't come on their own. Someone sent them and that person will pay.

# Chapter 33

*Devina*

⊪|||⊪ Bitter End – Gold Souls ⊪|||⊪

"I'm getting you out of here Vi. Baby please stay with me."
*Why does he sound so far away?*

Conned vision allows me to see Ryder's face but he's blurred. I'm being held by strong arms, but they aren't strong enough to keep me from drifting away.

"Get us to the car. We need to get to the hospital. Now!" he shouts. Moments later, tires screech to a halt and I'm being lifted into the back seat onto his lap.

"Baby, don't leave me."
*I can't leave you yet.*
*I changed my mind. I don't want to go.*

"We have so many more days to share. This can't be it." I want to say something, anything, so he knows I'm still here with him, but I feel so weak, and all I can manage is to bring my hand to his cheek. If only he knew, our days were already limited.

*I'm not ready.*
*I can't go.*

He won't get whatever revenge he was seeking if I die right now. I won't either. I should be using that to will myself to hold on, but the urge to let go is becoming greater. I can feel myself leave my body slowly. My mind is there, but I can't make my body do what I need it to.

I need to tell him I love him. I need to finish what I started and kill Cap. I reach aimlessly for my clutch which didn't make it to the car with me.

I need to last just a little longer. I need to love him just a little longer.

Part of my soul is being pulled toward Scarlet. She's so close, I can almost feel her.

# Chapter 34

*Ryder*

I grab her waving hand, which is already becoming cold, and press it to my cheek. I know her touch would be much more subtle and would feel like a whisper against my skin, but I want every ounce of her to feel that I'm here with her.

I bury my face in her hair and fight off the thought that I may lose her.

We pull up to the emergency doors and I exit the car with Devina in my arms, making a mad dash for the first doctor I see.

"She's been shot!" I shout in despair. It's only moments before I'm surrounded and Devina is being pulled onto a gurney. I'm holding onto her tiny hand like it's my lifeline.

*I can't let go.*

"Sir, you're going to have to let go. We can't help her if you don't let go." An older doctor places his hand on my shoulder in a gentle but firm tone. Before I can attempt to chase her, she's gone, taking my breath away with her.

# Chapter 35

## *Ryder*

Bad Habits – NERV

The waiting room is eerily quiet. I usually wouldn't wait in such an open space, but I need to make sure we don't draw too much attention. The fluorescent lights hum, taunting me, but it's better than being left alone with my thoughts.

"Here you go, Boss." Ronnie hands me a cup of coffee and sits to my right. Next to him is a bulletproof vest. Ronnie—always looking out for me.

I lean back and balance the plastic cup on my knee with a finger on top. "I want to know who called these orders." I stared straight ahead. I noticed the gauze over Ronnie's nose and knew that was my doing. Ruthlessly hacking up an enemy could bring such satisfaction, but knowing I smashed in his face when he was following my orders made me feel a hint of guilt.

"We're already on it, Boss. Looks like it may be the Russians." He seems unphased. Like I said, broken noses aren't uncommon in our industry. "The Russian made it out of the warehouse and he may be making another attempt to get to you through her. But I have to dig deeper." He stares forward pensively.

"I want them taken to the basement. The men can rough them up but I want them alive. Find out who the Russian is reporting to. He's not smart enough to be the head of this operation." I'm sure IT is the mastermind responsible for all of this.

Ronnie nods in acknowledgment and stands to leave. The adrenaline begins to leave me and I can feel my eyes becoming heavy.

The doctor clears his throat, waking me. As I try to regain my composure, my mind foggy, he takes a seat next to me and places his hand on my shoulder, almost bracing me for the worst.

"Your wife had a successful surgery Mr. Totaro, but her recovery is going to be longer due to her condition."

*She's going to be okay.*

"What condition? Is she pregnant? Did the bullet hit a lung?" I stand and wave dismissively to hurry him along. I just need to see my wife.

"No, the cancer, sir," he says as if to remind me. "She'll need to be handled very carefully. We were able to give her a transfusion, but she'll be in critical care for the next couple of days before we can let you take her home..."

His words hit with the same force of the bullet that struck my little sparrow and I stare down at the vests Ronnie left me as if they can somehow lessen the blow. The doctor's voice sounds loud but muffled as he continues without realizing that I've completely stopped listening.

*Cancer?*

I step back, trying to hide my reaction knowing that I can't possibly let anyone know that my wife has kept such a critical piece of information to herself.

I'll see her and she will clarify. This must be a mistake. My wife is twenty-three, vibrant, small but fierce. Her hair, she has it all. Her body, full of fucking sunshine. Her eyes are always full of such life and fire. It all replays in my mind at once. The glimpses of fear, the wall she's been so reluctant to let down, the bruises. She exposed it all to me but I was oblivious to what was right in front of me all along. Is this the secret her eyes have been hiding all of this time?

"You can see her now," he gently urges by pointing toward the door.

I don't know if I'm happy that she's alive, or if I'm devastated that I won't be able to protect her from the one thing that is killing her. Maybe I've reached a new level of fury that my body isn't capable of registering at the moment. I instinctively want to run to her side but my feet are weighed like bricks dragging through mud as I dread hearing any truth to what the doctor just told me.

I stop at the end of the hall and look into the room at my wife. The fluorescent lights try to hinder her beauty but her red lips and warm honey hair radiate strength. The machine next to her beeps and the nurse who is refilling her IV looks up at me with hopeful eyes.

"Your wife is a fighter, Mr. Totaro." She smiles as she walks past me out of the room. *You have no idea.*

I hesitate before stepping in, acknowledging now that the emotion I'm feeling is rage—at her for not telling me—for me being so blind to accuse her of unfaithfulness and spying while she suffered in silence. God, am I a bastard? There's still a chance that this is a mistake. I won't know until she tells me.

Gravity pulls me to her like it always does, perhaps even more so now than ever. But I don't know if the parts of me that are only holding together with scotch and nicotine will be able to withstand the blow of a truth that doesn't include her living the rest of my life with me.

She feels my presence and stirs in the bed, shifting her eyes to mine. I stop where I am, leaning against the door frame. She's terrified. She knows I know. *It's true.*

I have about three seconds to decide how I want to spend the rest of our time together. However much that is, I'm not sure yet, but I'm sure she's well aware.

Self-preservation used to be one of my stronger characteristics, but Devina seems to see right through me. Fortunately, this is a mirrored experience and there we stand, exposed to the elements of truth, tragically transparent.

# Chapter 36

*Devina*

He shifts his weight to lean against the door frame and lowers his head. I can't read him when he isn't looking at me. But then he does. He pulls his lips into a smirk, always trying to hide behind his sinful good looks. It would work if I didn't know him the way I do. His eyes meet mine again. Anger is prevalent, but the pain is there.

*He knows.*

"Ryder..." I try to plead with him but I can only make out his name before my stomach clenches and a sharp pain drives into my side causing me to wince.

He strides to me in two steps and takes my face between his hands. Strong and firm. His eyes pierce into me. Complete and utter devastation. He radiates anger and fury. He could snap my neck so easily and be done with me. Surely he won't kill me right here in this hospital, will he? Will he take me down to the basement?

I lied. I told him there was nothing else and *I lied.*

Maybe this is how it ends. In the hands of the man I love. I almost trust him enough to let it happen without a fight. His feelings for me will make it quick. I won't suffer. It will all be over. I can't think of a better way to go than in the arms of the man I love, although the thought of it happening at the will of his fingers is morbid and dark, and everything we are together. Seems like the perfect way to turn the page.

I don't have much time to think about it because his lips crash into mine and I feel hot liquid sprinkling onto my cheeks. I want to open my eyes, but I'm consumed. I can feel his tears and devastation. As his tongue slides over my bottom lip, I open to let him in. His kiss is one of rage and pain, and yet his lips hold mine like I'm a fragile piece of glass. His love is apparent and the betrayal of my secret cannot be denied.

"You're mine, Devina. I can't let you go," he says. I bring my hands to his and he stops to rest his forehead to mine. "How long?" he asks, eyes closed.

*How long have I known? Oh God, he's going to want to know everything.*

"How long do we have?" His words were as broken as his heart.

My heart weeps for us. We never had a chance.

I know I love him. But knowing doesn't bring sadness. Once I'm gone, I know I won't be missing anyone, and I'm grateful to experience any kind of love while I'm here. But it was easier to love him when I believed he didn't love me. Now there's no denying. The truth is he's been proving it every day in the mundane gestures of kissing me when I wake and making sure I'm never without a guard if he can't be the one with me. He proved it when he refused to leave me and when he shielded my body with his, just as I did for him.

His rage isn't toward me. He told me that he would burn the world down, and then put out the flame to keep me safe and unafraid. But he just realized that burning down the world won't save me.

His love cannot save me.

Nothing can save me, and as a man true to his word, he still thinks he needs to prove something to me.

I can only hope that the electricity in the air around us is enough for us to know that love is what will make these last moments matter. It all becomes too much and the medicine injected into my IV is starting to take hold.

My eyes flutter and I finally concede. "...Fly."

# Chapter 37

*Ryder*

⑪⑪⑪ Please Don't Go — Stephanie Rainey ⑪⑪⑪

*C*ancer.

Devina has cancer.

Devina is dying.

I can't save her.

She lies there exposed, hurting, shattered. Her hand is limp in mine as she sleeps. She wakes up every so often calling for me. I'm always here. I can't leave.

But she will.

I've replayed our time together on repeat. How did I miss the signs? There were signs. Not physically, but they're here. The way she hides from me while being completely exposed. The guardedness in her eyes.

I should hate her for lying to me. Has she been lying to me, or was she simply trying to endure?

I can't hate her though. I want to, which I'm sure is just as bad. But I love her more than the pain, more than the uncertainty, more than the fear of being without her.

For the day we made our vows, I picked her dress and flowers to match. I planned our wedding with the hopes of pleasing a woman I didn't know. And now, all too soon, I'll be planning a funeral for a woman I didn't have nearly enough time with.

She stirs, her eyes flutter open as she takes in the bleak hospital room. She needs to be reminded of where she is. The medication is making her foggy, but the doctor assures me it is necessary to manage her pain. Pain that I never knew she was feeling.

"Ry—" She tries to speak, but I'm standing at her side before she can finish, petting the hair away from her face.

"You had a long nap that time, sparrow."

The panic subsides and she leans into my hand. The sun has set, which marks our fourth night here. She's been too fragile to travel home, but with good news tonight, she'll be transferring in the morning.

"I don't know what to say." She releases a tear. I can't fault her. I have no idea what to say either.

"You don't have to say anything." I settle back in the chair next to her and prop my elbows on the bed to hold her hand in mine. Until her last breath, I'll make it my mission to hold her.

"You must be so mad." Her eyes shift to the ceiling, avoiding me.

"I'm not mad, Devina. I'm devastated. I'm trying to wrap my mind around the idea that when you leave, I'll have to survive even a moment without you before I get to find you again." I sigh. "It took me so incredibly long to find you."

"It wasn't supposed to be like this. I did this. We never had a chance."

Every word is true, but I won't hold it against her.

"Tell me what I can do," I beg. I need to do something other than sit in this fucking chair.

She's silent. We both know there's nothing I can do. There is nothing anyone can do.

She breaks her hand away from my grasp to reach for my cheek. I let her, pressing it firmly against my skin, memorizing the feeling.

There's only one question I have lingering, that I must know the answer to. "Are you scared?"

She smiles through her quiet tears. "No. I think death will be beautiful."

"Why is that?"

"Because people rarely come back."

My heart, which she mended, shatters to splinters. It will never be whole again.

# Chapter 38

*Devina*

When I wake again, Ryder is gone, but a familiar figure stands at the window gazing out.

"Taylor?" I squint. How did he find me?

"Hey sis, we've been really worried about you." He casually makes his way to me to plant a kiss on the top of my head. "Your husband will be right back. He's yelling at someone on the phone about your transfer home."

*Home.* I want to go home.

"How did you know where to find me?"

"I'm not sure what you told Ryder, but he called me from your burner. He told me to come. I don't think he knew that I was already privy to your medical diagnosis." He runs his hand through his shaggy black hair.

"I didn't push the button," I admit. "Something happened before we left, and when we did...well..." I gesture to all of me.

"Look, I know where your head is, but I think we need to consider calling it quits." He knows the words will rile me as he says them. He knows me too well.

"How can you say that to me? He has to pay for what he did."

"Be serious right now, Devina. You are *sick*. You can't put yourself in a bad situation again. Have you met your husband?" He sarcastically holds his hand out toward the door where Ryder is still on the phone on the other side. "He would kill me if he knew I kept helping you. He's already told me he wants to take care of it. I can't believe I'm saying this, but that guy really loves you, Vi."

141

"Why can't you believe it? Am I that unlovable?" I take a shot at a joke, but even a fake laugh hurts.

"Not at all. You know that. I just didn't realize…I didn't know it was real." He sits on the edge of my bed. "You know we both love you, right?" He stares at his hands in his lap.

"Ha! You're just saying that because I'm dying," I quip, rolling my eyes.

His head snaps my way, his pained gaze pierces through me. I know he loves me. I'll always love him. But I don't want to love anyone. I want to hate them all. Maybe then I can go peacefully. I can go with no regrets. I can just *go*.

"I think you know that's not true." His voice is sharp.

I nod. "I know. I'm sorry. You're the best friend I've ever had."

"Yeah, well when you get to the other side, let Scarlet know. That will piss her off." *There's my Tay.*

"She loved you too…" Speaking about Scarlet never gets easier, but I know it has to be said.

He nods.

Irish twins, they called us. So close, no words had to be said.

"She would have loved you too, Ryde," I call out to my husband who is now perched in the doorway.

"Sorry to interrupt. I wanted to give you two a moment." He steps to me, gazing down at me longingly.

"Any news about my departure?"

"The car will be here in fifteen minutes." He shifts his gaze from me to Taylor, assessing the relationship he doesn't yet understand.

My fingers trace his wedding ring when I realize my hand is bare.

"My rings! Where did they put them?" Ryder pulls them out of his pocket and gets down on one knee.

"I didn't get to ask the first time, sparrow, but would you be my bride?" He smiles up at me expectantly.

"Well, only if you're hellbent on being a widower." His smile falls. *Tough room.* "You guys have to lighten up. I can't spend the rest of my time being sad and scared," I complain.

"I think I speak for both of us when I say that losing you will cause an irreparable hole in our hearts." Ryder stands to place the rings on my fingers with much less enthusiasm now.

"I appreciate that. I appreciate you and you were so wonderful to ask Taylor to come. But once we leave this room, I want things to be as normal as possible." He raises a brow at me. "I mean it, Ryde, I don't want to spend a second more than I have to in doctor's offices and giving blood samples, being poked and prodded like a pin cushion. I want to sleep in my own bed. I want to run through our yard. I want to hang out with MaryClaire. I want—" His hand raises to make me pause.

"I want you to have everything you want. Why don't you make a list and I'm sure between the two of us, we can make it happen." He smiles. "Within reason, of course."

"Within reason..." I cautiously agree.

*Within reason, my ass.*

I'm still sore. I was shot.

The twenty-five-minute ride home felt like it took two hours. Ryder snapped at Leo every two minutes to drive carefully. Leo is my new Sal.

*Sal.*

He didn't even see it coming. I would cry for him again, but my body is now void of tears. I let the numbness take over. The physical pain is something I can manage. The rest. Well, the rest is something I'm not ready to face.

The past week has been filled with endless amounts of snacks being delivered every thirty minutes from Fiona. MaryClaire has visited twice bringing me coffee and donuts. Taylor visits throughout the day—every day.

Ryder won't leave my side. Ever.

Despite my endless protests, Ryder has hired several doctors from around the country to examine me. In our room. Our sanctuary.

I've obliged, knowing that once I'm gone, he'll have to continue living, and the least I can do is let him feel like he did everything he could to save me.

But nothing will save me.

I'm propped on pillows, waiting for my next appointment. Fiona sets my breakfast on my nightstand while MaryClaire sits next to me brushing my hair. Her quirky spirit has become something I look forward to. She reads me the latest stories she's been writing and I envy her creativity. One day, her work will be published, but I'm sure I won't be here when it happens. She's giving me all the juicy details of her and Ivan's romance while Ryder sits on the sofa by the window, reading.

"Hey, full house today." Taylor walks in carrying a box of pink stationery that I requested.

My room is buzzing with conversation. It feels odd to have all of my people together in one room while I lie propped on pillows in my pajamas.

A knock at the door causes everyone to pause and turn. Doctor Hammond. The poor man who has to deal with my husband today.

Ryder will sit at my side making sure the pricks don't hurt too bad and the doctor is making minimal contact with me. He'll stand at the foot of my bed, arms crossed, listening to the same information that Doctor Chavez gave us yesterday. The same information Doctor Reed gave us the day before.

But before all of that happens, I need everyone else to leave.

They take turns giving me a comforting pat on the arm, a wishful gleam in their eyes and words to attempt to ease my mind. Well, everyone but MaryClaire who tells me to let her know when the doctor leaves so she can come back and watch rom-coms with me.

It's nice to have a friend.

"Well, I think we know what the damage is, Doc. Can you

just give me an expiration date?" I ask, cutting straight to the point.

"Really, Devina?" Ryder is quick to finish closing the door before making his way back to my side.

"That is all I want to know. I don't want any more tests. I don't want any more doctors. I want to be done with all of this," I whine.

"Well, your injury didn't help at all, Mrs. Totaro," Dr. Hammond reports. As if I don't know. I still enjoy my name being said out loud.

"Obviously," I mutter to myself while Ryder chastises me with a stare.

"If you take precautions, I don't think your time will be shortened, but your quality of life may suffer as a result. I understand you're refusing care." He raises a brow.

I begin to talk until Ryder cuts me off. "Unless you believe there's a treatment that can help."

My blood boils. Crimson blurs my vision and I feel crescent moons pierce into my skin as I clench my fists.

"Enough!" Both men look at me in shock. "Enough. I need a moment with my husband."

Dr. Hammond nods before closing his chart and excusing himself.

We've been here before. Eyes locked, neither one wanting to back down.

I know he's mad. I know he wants to fix this, fix me, but nothing will. I've wasted a week. A precious week without vengeance, without breathing fresh air, without making a single damn decision about what I eat or wear. Specialists parade in and out of my room, poking and prodding me like a damn cow.

"Devina, what are you doing?" His voice is low and grave.

"I think the better question is what are *you* doing?" I hiss. "I told you I didn't want any of this."

"And I told you to be reasonable," he replies, crossing his arms over his chest, unwilling to see my perspective.

"This isn't reasonable, Ryder." I sigh, trying to regain my

composure. "This isn't how I want to spend my time. I need to get out of this house—out of this room! I need to walk in the garden and sit in the coffee shop. I need to see my brother." A different pain emerges when I realize Declan hasn't come to visit me.

Ryder makes his way to my side, bowing his head in defeat.

"I need to tell you about Michaela."

My breath freezes. Hearing her name spill from his mouth brings a wave of jealousy, but it quickly fades at the realization that there is no love in his eyes. Only disappointment.

"I was engaged before you," he begins. "We met young. Too young. But we were both raised with similar families and questionable morals. Her father worked for mine. There was no whirlwind romance, but I loved the idea of her. Hell, we were only together a handful of times, but back then, I thought she was the one." He runs his hand through his hair. I don't dare move. I need to know more. "That's how it started. Then her father started running drugs on the side. By the time I knew, it was too late. She was too far gone."

He stands and begins to pace. My mind reverts to the time I saw her last. She wasn't strung out. She was graceful and shone like the sun. I wanted to be beautiful like Hannah. Or Michaela. Whoever she was. When she walked into the room, men turned their heads in admiration.

"Our family never dealt with drugs. Only guns. He had been working for someone else." He pauses as I snap back to the present and try to fit the pieces together.

"Corman," I say, barely above a whisper.

He nods to confirm.

*My father.*

He's known this whole time. "How could you marry me? How could you agree to this after..." It clicks. Like a bullet dropping into the chamber. *Ryder wanted to ruin me.*

Bile burns in my throat and I can't stop what happens next. My gut heaves. Ryder is quick to grab the pail next to the bed before shoving it under my chin.

My head spins. "What happened to her?" I choke out.

"Her father called mine that night. Told us we needed to get to her before the Sullivans did. But we were too late. Cap was there when I arrived. He found her in a hotel room. The needle was still in her arm." *An overdose.* "I couldn't save her, Devina. I didn't even know until it was too late. She hid it so well." He lets out a heavy sigh, his eyes absent of any emotion. I knew that look. The look of someone who has relived death too many times and is now numb to its sting. The look of feeling nothing so you don't have to feel everything.

Guilt is a swift kick to my injured gut. *Like you hide things, Vi.*

He needs to know it all. To see the deepest parts of me. He doesn't want to save me. He *needs* to save me because he couldn't save her.

I need to talk to Declan. I have to know what happened between them.

I can still sense that something is wrong. That this wasn't the worst of it.

"You wanted to break *me*," I say more to myself than to him. Shame radiates from his skin.

"Cap didn't approve of our engagement," he goes on. "He was certain that she had found a lover. Our marriage was planned. It wasn't because we were madly in love. Hell, I wouldn't have been surprised if she had found a lover at some point. But we weren't even married yet. It was a fucking slap in the face. When I arrived, the room had been...used. She had been there with someone else."

*Declan.*

"Do you know who it was?" *I do.*

147

"I know you love your brother." That answers my question. "But when I look at him, I see the man who took everything that was supposed to be mine." *I see you, Ryder. I know your pain more than I can say.*

Understanding. Compassion. Pain.

It all hangs in the air around us.

"What do we do now?" I ask though I'm not sure I'll be able to stomach his answer. Will he want me to go back to Declan now? Is it too much to ask him to love me until he has to bury me?

"I wanted him to hurt the same way I did. I wanted him to pay for taking everything from me. But when I met you, everything changed. To hurt you would be to hurt a piece of me for something you didn't even do. I just couldn't do that to you. Now, I want to keep you with me as long as I can." He rasps with desperation in his voice. "I thought I knew pain and loss. I was angry for so long that I never got to say goodbye. But it didn't feel right." He adjusts himself on the bed next to me. Side by side, our fingers intertwine, the moment of silence building a tension I'm uncomfortable with.

"It didn't feel like I lost a part of me," he finally continues. "The disappointment and anger that came were real. But *almost* losing you, Devina, was like taking a bullet to the head."

His confession makes me question my own intentions and now I have an important question to answer. When the time comes, will I be able to make Ryder a casualty of war, for something *he* didn't do?

"This is why you want me to stop looking for the invisible man," I respond.

"I realized quickly that hurting you—hurting Declan—wouldn't bring her back," he says sternly. Ironically, the same words Declan had said before I married him. "And you and Declan shouldn't pay for your father's sins."

I have a choice to make.

A choice he can't know about.

And I don't know if I'm strong enough to make it.

# Chapter 39

*Ryder*

S haring my past with Devina brought more closure than anything. She has a presence that soothes me, though I could feel her tense at the mention of another woman's name.

The secrets we keep should tear us apart, but something greater is keeping us together.

I'm slowly letting go.

Not because I want to.

I want to hold on until it hurts.

But the frustration in her words hit me hard enough to knock some sense into me. She deserves whatever she wants. She thinks she wants to check things off a list before her time runs out. But I know she just wants to be able to choose.

Choose something for herself.

Choose anything.

But even on the hard days, she chooses me.

I've employed MaryClaire to stay with Devina while I catch up on the work I've been neglecting. The payment: two large pizzas and a scheduled Cold Stone delivery. The two are so very different, but MaryClaire makes Vi laugh and her spirits are visibly higher in her presence. I'm sure they'll both be equally high for the rest of the day since MaryClaire obnoxiously announced that she brought all the medicine Vi would need—two joints and her portable record player.

They were giggling like children as I left, but my heart felt lighter at the sound. A sound that doesn't frequent the walls of my home as it did only weeks ago.

Tonight I'm meeting with Declan to plan out our attack on the one they call IT. I could easily continue hating him. But the truth of the matter is—he didn't kill Michaela. Even if he did hand her the drugs, she made her own choices. Hell, I don't even know if he knows my involvement with her. I doubt it. If he did, he's even crazier than I thought for allowing me to marry his sister.

But tonight isn't about that. Tonight is about planning.

I arrive at our corporate headquarters fifteen minutes early. He's already here.

"How's my sister?" he asks, standing to greet me.

"She'd probably be better if you would check in on her." I start up my laptop and take a seat behind my oak desk.

He snuffs and stands to pour himself a drink from the cart. I don't know what his problem is. I can't stand that he hasn't even visited her. He has yet to step foot in our home. I can't for the life of me understand why he hates me so much. The ball is in my court, not his. He stole someone from me.

He pours two drinks and walks around the table to hand me a glass.

His glare fixates on the photo of Michaela I still have on my desk. I must have forgotten it was there. I haven't been to the office in weeks. "Why do you have a photograph of Hannah Buchanan?"

My eyebrows pinch as I shoot him a curious look. "You must be confused. Her name is Michaela."

"No. I think I would know my fiancé when I see her," he sets his glass on my desk—right next to the coaster. Asshole.

I look at him expectantly. He looks at me with the same frowned brows. Does he not know?

"You're kidding, right?"

He picks up the frame to examine the photo closer. "This is Hannah." His cheeks redden with frustration. "How did you know her? Do you know where she is?"

*The fuck?*

"Yeah, I know where she is." I roll my eyes as I lean back in my chair and prop one ankle up on the opposite knee.

He lets out a weighted sigh. "Well, next time you see her, tell her all is forgiven."

"I can't do that, Dec."

"What the fuck? Why not?"

"Declan, she's dead," I say cautiously, not knowing how he'll react.

The shock on his face is too real. He didn't know. This wasn't his work. "How?"

"Overdose. Three years ago."

He runs a hand down his face. Tears well in his eyes, but he looks to the ceiling to contain them. I know this look. I had it myself. It's hard not to cry for someone when the hate is equally matched with love or longing.

"You know I hated you for a long time, Declan." I break our silence.

"You mean your family hated my family."

I shake my head. "No. I mean I hated *you*."

He isn't sure how to respond. I don't know how to keep going. But I have to say it. I have to say it all.

"I was told it was you who was fooling around with her. That part I was willing to forgive. But the drugs." I take a moment to keep myself in check. "The drugs came from your family. We were supposed to get married and she overdosed on your family's drugs."

This is all new to him. The grief painted on his face mirrors the one I had on mine. My blackened heart wanted to crush him for what he'd done. But as he sits broken in front of me now, I don't feel any better. I feel worse.

He looks at me, his eyes searching mine. "I never gave her drugs. That part of the business ended when my father died."

"Well, how the hell do you think she got them, Declan? She was found with a fucking needle in her arm."

"Who found her?"

"Does it matter?"

"Yes. It does." He leans forward propping his elbows on his

knees, waiting.

"Her father. Her father called mine. He had been working for both of us. When I arrived, my father was there. He cleaned up the mess. The mess your family made," I accused.

"That can't be right, Ryder. By that time we were several years removed from anything of that nature. I hated having that near the girls. And after..." he trails off. "After the fire, I wouldn't risk having it near Vi."

This doesn't make sense. We sit like two idiots trying to figure out the missing piece to this puzzle. Michaela—Hannah—whoever the fuck she was, played us both, but someone gave her the heroine. It wasn't me, and now I'm learning it wasn't Declan.

Part of me is relieved that my wife's brother isn't as much of a prick as I originally thought. The other part feels like a god damn fool for wasting so much energy over the years on someone who's just as innocent as I am.

A knock at the door interrupts us. Ronnie enters with a manila folder. Declan and I give each other a knowing look. This conversation isn't over, but we have other business to take care of.

Photos of the mystery man we have been looking for. Ice blonde hair, bright blue eyes. I've seen this face before.

At the charity ball.

At the bar.

It was *him*.

"We have a location, Boss. What's the plan? We'll need all hands on deck. And not like that fucking container mishap. We need to be prepared this time. My guys tell me there are guns, but after seeing what they were selling last time..." He trails off not wanting to comment about the women we know are being sold and traded.

"Looks like the next 'shipment' is in three days," Declan says. "I'll let you run this. Tell me what you need."

"I can't run this. I know what's at stake, but I have Vi at home. My head isn't right," I say. "Ronnie, bring me whoever you can get your hands on tonight. Bring them to the basement. We'll see what we can get from them. This time, don't leave the fucking door open." I shoot him a pointed look.

His eyes light up like I just told him Santa came, dismissing my last instruction. He's always too eager to shed blood. "You got it, boss."

"We'll reconvene tomorrow morning. Devina and I will expect you at breakfast, Declan."

He nods, understanding the silent truce we just made.

# Chapter 40

*Devina*

Everything is lighter. I'm lighter.

MaryClaire's laughter floats around me.

I'm floating too.

Six slices of pizza and a split joint later, MC and I are at an all-time high.

"I'll admit he isn't as sinfully gorgeous as your husband, but he says all the right things...and *does* all the right things," she goes on about Ivan.

"Well, I'm happy for you. I didn't know what I was missing until I married Ryder. Once you find 'it' you should hold on for dear life. That kind of magic only comes along once in a lifetime."

"I know, I'm preaching to the choir. You're so lucky you have him." She props herself up on her elbows to give me the cheesiest smile.

"Oh yes, so lucky. I married a man I had never met and right when I fell for him, he found out I was dying of cancer." I roll my eyes.

"I don't mean to get heavy, but I have to ask. Why didn't you tell him?"

My heart aches at the directness of her question. I don't think it's something I even thought of myself. "I didn't *not* tell him on purpose. I didn't tell anyone but Taylor. I didn't want anyone to look at me like a piece of glass. I didn't want anyone to think I was weak," I admit.

"I get that." She lets my words marinate in her intoxicated mind. "What's the deal with Taylor anyway? Why didn't you ever hook up with that before you met Ryder? I give him a solid nine for looks." She giggles.

"Ew, no! We grew up together." I shove her arm playfully. "He's like my brother. I mean, not *my* brother, because my brother is distant and cold. But you know what I mean."

"Well, if I wasn't already planning a wedding in my mind with Ivan, I would definitely go after someone like Taylor," she muses.

"He's got his own baggage. He's sullen and dark. And you're light and rainbows." I laugh. "That would be an interesting match."

"Too bad we'll never know." She throws a piece of pepperoni my way and pulls herself off the floor to change the record.

A knock at the door has us hiding our stash under the bed before Fiona peeks her head in. "Your ice cream order arrived." She beams as she steps into the room. Sniffing the air, she gives me a pointed look. "Well, it smells like you all are having a good time in here."

We make a poor attempt at containing our laughter before we're both rolling around on the floor.

"Join us, Fiona!" I say as she sets the ice cream on the blanket we've laid out. "You work for my husband; you deserve a little break."

"He can be a handful." she rolls her eyes. "What the hell, let me at it." We cheer and hand her a joint.

The atmosphere is serene. My large room spins around us as we lay on the floor, our heads together. *Strawberry fields forever* plays in the background. The Across the Universe version. My favorite.

For a moment, I forget I'm sick.

I hadn't realized that I wasn't really living until I accepted that I was dying. My body is no longer laced with ice.

*This is what real friendship feels like.*

This is what acceptance feels like.

This is what home feels like.

I haven't felt this close to anyone since Scarlet. I've spent years avoiding friendships and people in general. No one could take Scarlet's place, but sharing in laughs that didn't include her, making memories without her, not being able to share experiences with her... each felt like a tiny betrayal. A step away from everything I wanted to hold on to.

But as I lie here right now, stoned out of my mind, full of pizza and ice cream, I relish the feeling of camaraderie with the women on either side of me. If I didn't know better, I'd say Scarlet worked her magic from beyond the grave to send these beautiful souls to me in my time of need.

I have to stop believing that I can't be the recipient of love just because I'm not always capable of giving it.

I let my mind drift. When the darkness consumes me, I welcome it.

Large arms lift me from the floor. I know it's Ryder before he speaks. His scent is one I'll never forget. His embrace is filled with tenderness and strength.

"I assume you had a good time tonight, sparrow?" he coos. I smile. My eyes are too heavy to meet his, but I know I'm smiling.

He places me gently in the bed, but I don't feel the mattress dip. "Don't leave me." I lazily reach out a hand, which he kisses.

"I'll be up shortly, love. I have some business to take care of downstairs. I'll be up before you know it. Just sleep." Silk and sleep cover me.

This is what peace feels like.

This is what love feels like.

The hair on my arms stands at attention before my mind catches up to the sound echoing through the walls.

*Bang!*

My eyes, still heavy, are forced open from fear. I'm frozen.

*It's a dream, Devina. He can't get you.*

The crack of gunfire rings out again.

Not a dream.

Reaching across the bed, I find nothing but cold sheets. Ryder isn't here. I need to run.

*Run Devina!*

I force myself past fear and kick my legs over the side of the bed. I tiptoe over to the door, listening, but there's only silence.

Peering out, I find the hallway to be dark. No footsteps. No commotion.

I can't stay here. The first place someone would look is my bedroom. That's exactly what happened last time.

Flashbacks threaten to take me to the dark place in my mind that I keep under lock and key, but I have to remain here. In the present. I have to get out.

I press myself against the wall and slide, making my way to an empty bedroom on the other side of the stairs. My eyes are adjusting to the darkness. There's nowhere to hide. Perhaps under the bed. I roll my eyes knowing that's the first place someone would look, but it's the only place I have right now. I should have picked a better room.

I lower myself to the ground, trying not to make noise. I'm healed, but the weight of my body causes my stomach to tense and a whimper to escape my lips. I slither under the bed and close my eyes.

Waiting.

Minutes feel like hours, but I don't dare move.

Footsteps climb the staircase. Once at the top, they grow

faint. They're heading to my room. I silently pat myself on the back for being brave enough to leave when I did.

A door slams. And another. And another.

"Devina!" A deep familiar voice echoes through the halls.

*Ryder.*

My cries lead him straight to me.

The door swings open and light illuminates the room. His feet walk toward me, but I'm still frozen. He gets down on his knees and leans to peer under the bed at me.

"Vi, what are you doing in here?" Concern laces his voice as he reaches for me.

I'm a brave girl. I can come out now.

I take his hand and let him guide me out from under the bed. My chest heaves but I'm still trying to process what happened.

"I heard a gun. I thought it was..." I can't even say the rest out loud, but I don't need to. He knows what I thought. My puffy eyes leak tears down my cheeks.

"You're safe now. I'll keep you safe." He pulls me close, lifting me with ease. "I've got you," he continues to soothe.

Walking back to our bedroom, he climbs into bed before setting me down. He undresses, his eyes never leaving mine.

"Why are you looking at me like that?" I curl into a ball, embarrassed.

"You scared me, sparrow. I didn't know what to think when I didn't find you where I left you." He slides down next to me, pulling me close. "I can't take my eyes off you now."

"Was that a gun? Who was shooting at you?"

"Who said they were the ones shooting?" He lifts a brow and looks down at me like I said the silliest thing.

I shouldn't be surprised, but I am. The two sides that make Ryder Totaro are so far apart. I'm reminded that there's a part of him he refuses to let me see.

I can't be mad. But I wonder if that's the reason he allows me to keep part of my secret. He knows it'll hurt him, just as his secrets can hurt me.

I nuzzle into his shoulder as his fingers trace my arm. His

scent calms me. His warmth soothes me. I hold him close, allowing our breaths to sync.

"You're safe," he reminds me. "Nothing can take you from me."

*I wish so much for that to be true.*

But I let myself believe it, just a little longer as sleep takes us.

# Chapter 41

*Ryder*

S he sleeps, but I can't.

My heart dropped when I walked into our room and found an empty bed. The fear of having lost her was heavy enough to bring me to my knees.

She's here. She's in my arms. But time is a thief. Cancer is a thief. Nothing will keep her with me. So I lie here, memorizing her shallow breaths, the flutter of her lashes as she dreams. Her honey-red hair spays across the pillow. Her lavender scent feels like home.

I wonder how I'll survive. How I'll draw breath after she exhales her last?

She stirs in my arms, her gaze climbing my chest until her eyes meet mine.

"How long have you been watching me sleep?" Her cheeks heat.

"Not long," I lie.

"I'm going to miss this." She reaches her hand up to cup my jaw.

I should be saying the same to her. "How do you know you'll even be able to miss me where you're going?" I chuckle.

"Maybe we don't get to go anywhere when we die. Maybe we just go back to the beginning and start again," she ponders out loud.

I've never given much thought to death, and when I think of it now, I become enraged at the thought that it's the only thing

I can't conquer for her.

"That would be something, wouldn't it?" She nods in agreement. "Well, when we start over, let's start when we met. That's the moment I began living in this life." I pepper her face with kisses as she scrunches her nose. "I vow this to you, my little sparrow, the moment my eyes close for the last time, I'll find you in the darkness."

Her chuckle dances around us. "How can you find me in the dark?"

"Because you're the light."

Her expression becomes somber. "Maybe I'm not the light. Maybe you can just see in the dark."

My eyes search hers. I want to ask why she can't see herself the way I do, but I don't.

Her soft smile returns, but her eyes remain glazed. "Promise you'll come for me?"

"I will always come for you, Sparrow." I kiss the top of her head. "I promise."

We're sitting in the sunroom when Fiona announces Declan's arrival.

Devina straightens in her chair. She's hurt, but she'll do everything she can to hide it from him.

He rounds the table to plant a kiss on the top of her head. "Vi, I'm happy to see you're doing better."

"How nice of you to make time to visit." The sarcasm drips from her lips like the syrup she's pouring on a pancake.

Her hair lies in waves down her back. Her yellow sun dress gives the illusion that she's vibrant. The truth is that her glow is slowly fading. She's still radiant. Her smile is brighter than the sun. But her eyes are becoming tired.

Declan ignores her comment and takes a seat across the table.

"We need to finish our discussion, Ryder," he says.

Devina looks between us curiously.

"There seems to be some confusion as to whether Michaela was someone named Hannah," I catch her up.

"I know," she mutters.

"What do you mean, 'I know'?" Declan demands.

"Taylor was looking into Ryder when we first got married. We didn't know what it meant." She sips her coffee. "I wasn't sure what the story was but I let it go. Until Ryder told me what happened."

"So you knew when I told you?" Why did she keep this from me?

"I didn't know everything. I just knew she was a shady woman, and frankly, I didn't want to know that much about one of your exes. I had no idea how complicated it all was," she says calmly.

Declan and I stare between each other and Devina, who has written the entire situation off.

"What I want to know is where she got the drugs. Something is off. I didn't even know that was an issue. And now I find out you weren't dealing." I look to Declan. "What happened the last time you saw her?"

"She wasn't on drugs, I can promise you that. She would have never touched them." He pours himself a cup of coffee. "The last time I saw her she was happy. She said she was going upstate to visit her father. I didn't hear from her after that. She ignored my calls and I let it go. After our family died, I had to keep things together for Devina. I couldn't be distracted."

Devina closes her eyes slowly, taking in his words as if realizing for the first time that she's important to him.

"Someone gave her the drugs," I conclude. "I agree, she would have never touched them. I guess we have two choices. We can let it go or we can look into who gave them to her."

Declan shifts in his chair. "Honestly, I think we have enough on our plates right now. Finding anything out about her isn't going to bring her back. She was involved with people she shouldn't have been dealing with."

I look at Devina and know the last thing she wants is for me to be deep-diving into my ex's potential murder.

"Well, that's that. If Devina has taught me anything, it's that time is precious and should not be wasted." I reach my hand to caress her thigh. She blushes at the gesture. "We're on the same team now, Declan. It's about time we start acting like it."

"Agreed." Declan's gruff voice is deep with a hint of sadness. I can't be so selfish to think I'll be the only one suffering once she's gone. She may very well be the only form of light that idiots like us get to experience.

"What we can do is decide how we're moving forward with the Bratva. We have two more days..." Devina stabs a piece of sausage on her plate, a little too aggressive. "Perhaps you can relax in a bath while Declan and I hash out the details." I bring her knuckles to my lips. She's hesitant, but she rises to leave.

"Declan." She turns back to the table. "Please come by more. I've missed you." Sadness laces her voice.

"Promise," he says.

# Chapter 42

*Devina*

Overhearing part of their plan from the other side of the door made me uneasy. My brother and my husband are planning to storm a warehouse full of men who will have one mission: to kill them. Maybe it's because I know the softer side of each of them and I've only heard the worst about the Bratva, but the thought of losing them both is enough to make me heave.

Settling into the bath, I try to rid my mind of the chaos that is about to ensue, when my phone pings with a message from MaryClaire.

> **MaryClaire: Ivan left me. I need you. Can you come to my apartment?**

> **Me: Ry will want to come too. He won't let me out of his sight…unless you can come here?**

> **MaryClaire: No. I need you to come here. Alone.**

> **MaryClaire: Girl stuff.**

MaryClaire has been so good about coming over. I want to reciprocate the gesture she's made for me, but I'm at a loss for what to say to Ryder. Maybe I can just slip out while he's distracted with Declan.

> **Me: Give me a few minutes and I'll head over. Hang in there, girl.**

Toweling off, I see my reflection in the mirror. I can't remember the last time I examined my scars. I feel smaller. My body is weaker, but only slightly. But I also feel beautiful. These scars are fading. Maybe not on my skin, but on my heart.

I get dressed quickly in a pair of leggings and a soft hoodie. Mentally planning my argument, I head down the stairs. *MaryClaire needs me. She's my best friend. She's been there for me. I need to be there for her. I'm a grown woman!*

That's it.

Lay on the guilt so I can get there quickly and without a chaperone.

Hitting the bottom of the stairs, I pause to soak in the silence. No one is here. They must be in the basement. The one place I'm not supposed to go.

I send a text that I'm heading to MaryClaire's and sneak out the front door before anyone can stop me. She lives above the coffee shop in town. I text her that I'll be there in twenty minutes.

When I walk up to MaryClaire's apartment, I'm not surprised that her front door is unlocked. I hear the shower running and stuff my phone in my coat pocket before shrugging it off and laying it over the dinette chair. "Hey girl, I'm here!" I holler. "Is it too early for wine? I'll open a bottle. It sounds like you need it."

The living room light illuminates the open space as I reach for two wine glasses and spin around to begin my "he doesn't deserve you" speech but I'm met with a massive mountain of a man with striking blue eyes and bright blonde hair. The glasses are dropped and shattered as I push myself back against the counter.

"She knew you'd come." His voice is ice cold. From MaryClaire's descriptions, I know this is Ivan.

My eyes dart around the small apartment, looking for evidence of MaryClaire, for a weapon, for my phone—which is in my coat pocket across the room from me.

"Where is she?" I demand, although I'm pretty sure it only came out as a whisper.

"You can calm down. I need you alive...for now." He tips a bottle over a rag and takes his first step toward me. The bathroom is closer than the front door. I just have to get through the door and I can go out the fire escape.

I make my move and lunge trying not to fall on the shattered glass but he's too fast. He grabs my arm and I fall forward, head first into the door. My ears ring and a sharp pain shoots down my neck.

"I wouldn't have taken you as a fighter," he taunts. I kick. I scratch. I scream.

The rag presses down on my face and everything fades to black.

# Chapter 43

*Ryder*

·ılı|ılı· In The Air Tonight – Natalie Taylor ·ılı|ılı·

My phone pings with a text from Devina. She's going to MaryClaire's. Moving to stand, Declan stops mid sentence to ask where I'm going.

"My wife has decided to leave. Likely on her own again." I pinch my fingers between my brows. This woman is infuriating.

Declan pulls up his phone. "Where does MaryClaire live?"

"Above the coffee shop in town," I answer.

"Yeah, she's just getting there now." He shows me his screen. A blue light making its way to MaryClaire's house.

"You are tracking *my wife*?" I ask in disbelief.

"No. I'm tracking *my sister*." He shrugs as if it's the most normal thing in the world.

I roll my eyes and sit back down. "Fine. But I want whatever you have on her phone removed before you leave. I'll go get her when we're finished."

He lets out a low chuckle. "Whatever you say, man."

God, I want to give him one good punch to the mouth. But I won't. Right now I'm grateful that I know where she is.

An hour later we're wrapped up and I head over to MaryClaire's to grab Devina.

When I reach the top of the stairs I see the door open. I peer inside to see shattered glass. I call Devina's phone only to hear it ring on the chair next to me.

My next call is to Declan.

"I think Devina has been taken." I try to control my voice.

"Hold on, I'll track her."

"You can't track her. I'm holding her fucking phone." I roll my eyes.

"You think I put it on her phone? *Please.*" I can hear him roll his eyes right back at me. "Was she wearing her claddagh ring?" he asks.

"She never takes it off," I recall.

That son of a bitch had a tracker on her this entire time.

"We have a problem." He jumps back on the line. "She's on her way to the docks. I'll call Taylor. Is MaryClaire there with you?"

"No, but it looks like one or both of them put up a fight. There's broken glass everywhere."

A heavy sigh travels through the phone. "Hopefully they're still together. And alive."

"I'll call Ronnie. Call Taylor and have him meet us there."

Fear pierces through me. Rage boils beneath the surface until it explodes as I flip the table in front of me. They have my sparrow. But why? What use is she to them? They could have easily come for me or any one of my companies. It seems like a huge overstep.

But right now I need to get to the docks. I need to get her back.

I pull up to where I see Declan and Taylor. Ronnie isn't far behind, arriving on his bike.

The last time I was here, I set off a bomb that nearly killed me. This time, we don't know which container she's in. Fuck, she might not even be on one. Declan fumbles with his phone to try and nail down her location.

"She's there." He points. But the general location is a freight boat with hundreds of containers. "I can't tell if she's in the boat or one of the containers on top." He's frustrated. So am I. I try not to kill him for not knowing exactly where she is. His fucking tracker is useless.

"Spread out, case the area. Don't take anyone out if you can help it. I don't want any attention drawn to us," I instruct.

Taylor runs his hands through his hair. I can tell he's been crying. It pains me to see him mad to the point of tears. He truly loves Devina, but he's not in his element. He's the man behind the scenes, or so it would often seem. While he's an amateur in this arena, I know he'll fight to the death to get back what is mine.

We spread out, slowly making our way to the large boat.

The damp sea air makes my shirt cling to my skin as I sling toward the blue light on the screen. I listen for her voice, her scream, anything.

*I'm coming for you, sparrow. I'll always come for you.*

# Chapter 44

*Devina*

M y head throbs. My eyes are opening, but I can't see. A dull light is in the distance, but blackness is all around. I can smell the ocean. The salt pricks my nose, making me aware of where I am. We have to be close to the docks. There's a body next to me.

It's warm.

It's heavy, draped over one of my legs.

I want to move, but my limbs are heavy and stale. My hands clasped together with plastic. I try to shift from under the weight and my hand grazes someone's hair. Curly hair.

*MaryClaire.*

Trying to push her awake, she stirs and lets out a small moan. *She's breathing.* If I don't make it out of here alive, I can't take her with me to the other side. I have to fight.

Heavy footsteps echo as a large form blocks out the light for a moment before drawing near.

Stopping only feet away from me, he reaches up to pull the string hanging next to a bulb, illuminating the space around me. I squint to adjust my eyes.

MaryClaire's eyes flutter open. Our gazes meet and she pushes herself up to sit next to me against the wall behind us. She's confused. Unaware of where she is.

*Same, girl.*

"Did my sleeping beauties have a nice rest?" Ivan asks, but he doesn't wait for an answer. "You two will sell for higher than our usual merchandise." He raises a brow.

"My husband will be coming for me and when he does he'll fucking gut you," I spit.

"Your husband is the least of my concerns. In fact, he's not of any concern." He licks his teeth. "Your brother, on the other hand, is someone I'm very interested in getting my hands on."

"What did my brother ever do to you?" I ask, trying to rack my brain to retrieve any recollection of this man with my brother.

"He took something from me. Cost me millions." He straightens his back, peering down at us.

"Well, if you're looking for payback, you picked the wrong girl. My brother doesn't even know I'm here and I doubt that he'll care." The words hurt as I say them because they ring true.

He smirks.

"So you're going to kill me?" I ask, wondering if he even knows I'm just as likely to die on my own before Declan or Ryder could ever find me.

"Oh no, princess. I'm going to sell you to the highest bidder." My blood runs cold. "Your family has created a lot of enemies over the years. Enemies who would pay a great amount to take their turn breaking you."

MaryClaire, who's been awake but silent, shifts against the wall, leaning closer to me. I reach for her hand and we sit, marinating in the fear his words peppered over us.

"Try not to do anything stupid while we wait, princess. I won't kill you"—he places the gun he's been holding in the back of his black slacks—"but I will make you wish you were dead. They don't call me Ivan the Terrible for nothing."

With that he turns on his heels and walks out of the room, slamming a metal door.

MaryClaire is the first to break. Her tears are warm as they fall on my arm. Cradling her head and petting her hair, I look around the room to find a different point of entry.

"How original." I roll my eyes. "He had to use someone else's nickname."

"I'm so sorry Vi. I didn't know he'd do this," she says between sobs. "He's going to fucking sell us? What does that even mean?"

I know what it means, but MaryClaire isn't from our world. I hate the idea that her first introduction was so cruel.

"It's okay. We just have to do what he says for now. I know Ryder will come. He won't let anything happen to us."

I want so much for those words to be true, but doubt drips in.

Hours seem to pass but perhaps it's just the endless dripping of a pipe that makes the time move at a glacial pace. We sit mostly in silence, aware of what's on the other side of the door. I'm convinced there's some kind of camera in this room, allowing them to watch us. I saw no other men, but it would be foolish to believe Ivan is working alone. Men like him don't do the dirty work themselves, they have people to do it for them.

"If I don't make it out of here," MaryClaire breaks the silence, "I just want you to know you're my best friend." Her voice is void of emotion. She's not herself. I doubt either of us will ever be again.

"I told you already. Ryder will be here soon," I argue. "We're both getting out of here." I pause before saying something I don't want to say but have to be brave enough to mean. "If it comes down to me or you, I want you to run. You have to leave me."

She shakes her head vigorously. "I could never leave you. And I know you would never leave me. We're going to get through this together."

Her words are filled with determination and hope. Right now, I have neither. If I were here alone, I could handle this. But she's right. I could never leave her.

The lock on the door clinks and the door swings open. A man

I've never seen enters carrying a tray. He's silent as he walks to the table on the far wall and sets down a tray of food.

"How long are you planning on keeping us in here?" I ask.

Silence.

"Where are we?" I ask.

Silence.

I roll my eyes in frustration. He makes his way back to the door and gives me a look over his shoulder.

"You'd be wise to eat. He won't let you out until you do." His accent is thick and threatening.

Is he going to let us out? If he is, that means he must be moving us to another location. He's not letting us out to wander this ship—which is where I assume we are. The walls, metal. The door has a circular window about the size of my face.

I twist my wrists only to chafe my skin against the corner of the sharp plastic tie. Even if we get out of this room, I have no clue how to get out of *here*.

MaryClaire stands to retrieve our tray. Sitting back next to me, we rip apart the peanut butter sandwiches and cautiously eat.

"Wouldn't it be a kick to the balls if I were allergic to peanuts?" I quip and see a smirk rise on her face.

"How can you possibly make jokes right now?" she asks.

"Easy, if I don't, I might just die from anxiety. And since I can't die and leave you alone in here, I have to voice the joke when it comes."

"But you will leave," she whispers, and I know her words have nothing to do with our current predicament.

Placing my sandwich back on the plate, I grab her hands in mine. "I'll miss you so much. But my time isn't up yet. Only I get to say when that happens and it's not happening tonight."

"Well, you don't get a say." She side-eyes me. "But I like your enthusiasm. What do you have in mind?"

Gazing down to MaryClaire's signature pink pumps, I have an idea. She must read my mind. Her eyes shoot back up with anxiety.

"Oh no, they're my favorite," she whines.

I have to bite back a laugh. That's the MC I know and love.

There's only one way out of here and I'm not going down without a fight.

# Chapter 45

*Devina*

Huddled in the corner, we wait until our captor returns. The same man who brought us food returns for the tray and places water bottles on the table.

"Good girls," he says as he examines our empty tray. Ryder uses those words to praise me, but coming from this oaf, I want to burn my ears off.

As he turns to leave I make my move, pushing myself off the floor and sprinting toward him. My heart is beating so fast but the world around me slows down.

I shove him into the door, which only stuns him. He's on me before I can retreat. His hands clench around my neck. I'm choking on my spit, one last attempt to tell him to fuck off. *I always have to have the last word.*

"You fucking bitch," he screams as his upper lip curls, baring his teeth.

With his weight on top of me, my fight is fleeting and my hands involuntarily become lax around his writs. Just as the blackness threatens to take over, I see MaryClaire approach. She winds up and aims, kicking his head like a soccer ball. He falls back as the blood begins to pour from his nose.

MaryClaire's eyes meet mine. The rabid look in her eye both impresses and terrifies me as she breaks our gaze to lunge for his gun.

He raises a hand, keeping one on his nose, as he chuckles to himself. "Sweetie, you have no idea what you're doing. Give me the gun and we can forget this ever happened."

Her finger is glued to the trigger. Her tethered hand cups the base of the gun. I know she can shoot him now and it'll be over. When more men come, which we can only assume they will, we'll take as many as we can as we push our way out of here.

That's the plan.

But MaryClaire's eyes grow double in size as he slowly pushes himself off the floor, now towering above us.

"Give me the gun, sweetheart," he urges.

"Fuck you," MaryClaire spits back as she closes her eyes to pull the trigger.

Everything slows around us as he lunges toward her. Instinctively I do too.

The gun goes off, echoing the walls around us as we all fall to the floor.

# Chapter 46

*Ryder*

A gunshot rings from below deck. I duck behind a crate as three men jog toward the shot.

I can sense her. She's close. I find Taylor, crouched at an entrance. He lifts his finger to his mouth to shush me. My heart is pounding. What if that bullet was for her?

He peeks down the corridor, satisfied with the distance between us and the men. He gives me a nod to proceed.

Shoulder to shoulder, we line up and take our shots. Three shots. Three assholes down. The metal walls reverberate the sound and I can feel it in my bones. Inching down the hallway, we come to the last door.

Two pathways branch off on either side, but I know she's in here. I peer in the window to see auburn hair spread across the floor and my heart sinks. I burst in to find Devina and MaryClaire lying on the ground, covered with a man and the blood that is still oozing from his body.

I rush to her, brushing the hair away from her face. Taylor sits beside me checking MaryClaire's pulse.

"Vi, I'm here. Please get up baby," I plead.

Her lashes flutter until her eyes gradually open. *There's my girl.* MaryClaire begins to cough next to her.

They're both alive.

*They're alive,* I chant to myself.

I pull Devina up by her shoulders until she's seated in my lap and begin examining her for injuries. Her hands are bound. Taylor opens a switchblade to release the girls. The moment

Devina's hands are free, she throws her arms around my neck. "I knew you'd come," she whispers against my ear.

I want to hold her close. I never want to let go. I press her to me knowing I won't be satisfied until we're one. But we have to go. *Now.*

"It was Ivan," MaryClaire says as she looks up at Taylor. I don't know much about her, but I know she's never experienced our world and she's likely in shock from it all based on how calm she is.

I help Devina to her feet as Taylor scoops MaryClaire up in his arms. We begin to make our way to the hall and aim for the door we entered from.

Nearly there, we halt at the sight of a large figure blocking our exit, but let out a sigh of relief when we realize who it is.

*Declan.*

"Christ," he murmurs, taking in the sight of the women latching onto us.

"Let's go," I bark as we burst past him.

Shots ringing out from our right force us to turn left and away from the ramp leading back to the dock.

Nearing the front of the boat, we run out of places to go. Turning around to assess an escape route, I see that we're nearly surrounded. I tuck Devina behind me, shielding her from the assholes standing before us.

Ivan makes his way through an army of men, his heavy boots hitting the floor with a stomp.

"Declan Sullivan," he purrs. "I see I finally got your attention."

"What exactly do you want, Ivan?" I ask, as Declan and I look at each other curiously. *What does this have to do with Declan?*

"The Sullivans took something from me six years ago," he begins his taunting, pulling a large blade from his belt. "Your father was a lot easier to control back in the day. But you, well you didn't even care when your precious Hannah was taken."

Declan's face pales and my ears ring.

"You gave her the drugs," Declan says with confidence.

Ivan chuckles. "I wouldn't have had to send a message if you hadn't cut off my business!" he shouts into the night sky like a fucking maniac. His eyes seer into Declan like a rabid animal that needs to be put out of its misery.

His men stand at attention, waiting for instruction. Devina's nails pinch my skin as she holds on for dear life.

The slight motion of a shadow pulls my eyes to the right. Ronnie sits on top of a crate with his shot lined up.

"It looks like I got more than I intended when I picked up your sweet baby sister. Good thing he spared you before setting that fire, princess," he says to Devina, and she becomes stiff behind me.

"What do you mean *he*?" I ask.

"Oh, you don't know? It would seem you Totaros are keen on keeping secrets in the fam—" He stops as a bullet strikes his shoulder.

Gunshots erupt as his men turn to fire back toward Ronnie. Declan and I pull out our guns, taking out the men closest to us while Taylor pulls the girls away behind a wooden crate. "We have to jump!" he shouts at them.

I look back, connecting with Devina, nodding for her to go, but I know she won't leave without me.

"Don't you fucking dare, Devina!" I shout back toward her before aiming at my next victim. The last thing I need is her trying to take another bullet for me, but I can see it painted on her face that she's more than willing.

One by one, Ivan's men drop. Bodies collect at our feet as Declan and I inch forward.

Familiar faces appear before me and I realize Ronnie must have called in the calvary.

Ivan's been shot but he pulls himself away.

"Not so fucking fast." Declan approaches him, gun drawn. "This is for Hannah." He doesn't wait for a reply as he pulls the trigger, exploding the back of Ivan's head across the deck. He kicks him with his shoe to roll him over.

I've done my fair share of torture, but this is grotesque and barbaric. Gray matter splattered inches away from my feet. I fight the urge to vomit.

Our men push the remaining army to their knees, waiting for instruction. It only takes me a moment to decide. They hurt my sparrow. They tried to destroy her, take her from me. They all must die.

I nod to Ronnie, who then gives the order. In unison, my men fire, leaving the remaining men in a pile in front of us.

I turn to see Devina peering around the crate. I've tried to keep this all from her. I tried to shelter her, just as Declan had in the past. But I know that if I don't want to add to her nightmares, she'll need to see our enemies dead at her feet to be convinced they won't come back to hurt her.

MaryClaire, who has finally come back to reality, marches toward Declan. Staring down at Ivan, she lifts her foot and drops it intentionally onto his face, stabbing him through the eye with her heel.

"I just had to make sure," she says as one of our men succumbs to the urge to hurl.

# Chapter 47

*Declan*

MaryClaire's shoe yields pieces of Ivan's brain as she turns to walk back to Taylor. He wraps his arm around her protectively. Ryder seeks out Devina and pulls her into a tight embrace.

My eyes scan the layer of death that has been sprinkled on the deck. This is my fault. This is *my* fault.

Hannah.

Scarlet.

Devina.

I couldn't save them. I can't save them. I brought this on us all because of the fucked up world we live in. The world our fathers created for us to reign.

This has to end.

"Take the girls," I order Taylor and Ryder. "I'll get this cleaned up."

Walking past me, Devina pauses to look up at my face. She's resilient. A vision of grace. Pure fire, but a graceful one. Reaching up, she scratches the hair on my jaw. This time, I don't shy away. I pull her into my arms and look up, silently thanking whoever is responsible for keeping her safe. It sure as hell wasn't me.

# Chapter 48

*Ryder*

I got her back, but for how long?

Each day is becoming bleaker. MaryClaire, Taylor and Declan are now staying in our house.

MaryClaire was too traumatized to go back to her apartment. I don't blame her. It was a shit apartment anyway. We'll figure something out eventually, but for now, she wants to be with her friend, and I won't stop her.

Taylor and Devina have the kind of relationship I know she wants so desperately to have with Declan, but it's been one formed over decades. Unfortunately for Declan, he'll never have that with her. He still stays, hoping she'll be coherent enough to forgive him, or even hear him out.

The guilt is painted on his face. How the hell was he supposed to know about the shady shit his father was working on? In our line of work, everyone assumes you are in on the information. That's not always the case. It's not his fault Corman was a horrible father and worse boss. It's not his fault Michaela is dead—as much as I still feel the need to lay blame.

We've been hosting family dinners almost every night since we found the girls on the boat. I want every second of my time to be consumed with her. Her scent. Her laugh. The way she looks at me. But I need to share her. They'll miss her too. Not like I will, but still. She's the force that brought us all together. She's the thread that binds us. When she's gone, they'll only have each other.

She scoops mashed potatoes onto her plate and throws her head back in laughter at something MaryClaire said.

"Can you knock it off already?" Taylor scruffs from the other side of the table.

"I don't know, Taylor," MaryClaire teases. "I think you should really consider turning those computers off and joining us in the real world more often. You might even find a woman out in the wild instead of a pixilated sorceress." The girls giggle.

Taylor rolls his eyes, but I can tell he enjoys the banter. He lets MaryClaire egg him on just to enjoy Devina's laughter a little longer. Internally, I'm just as desperate as he is for the sound.

"You two should just get a room already!" Devina smiles, poking MaryClaire's arm.

MaryClaire blushes, looking away as Taylor squares his shoulders, shifting in his seat.

"Oh god, I was kidding." Devina laughs as the rest of us have grown quiet. "It wouldn't take long before you kill each other."

"I wouldn't kill you MaryClaire," Taylor assures her with a wink and a smirk.

"Yeah, but being stuck with you might drive me to kill myself." She tosses a fry at him and everyone chuckles again.

The rest of the evening is spent in the family room as the girls fight us over a movie to watch. As if we had any chance of winning. Devina will have whatever she wants for as long as she wants. Tonight, she wants to watch 'We Bought a Zoo'.

She falls asleep ten minutes into the movie and everyone makes their farewells, heading up to their rooms, leaving me alone with her and my thoughts.

She still doesn't know who killed her sister and it seems it's the only closure she seeks before the cancer consumes her. I've vowed to make them pay—once we find out who the fuck it is.

I'll kick down every door and burn down every city to make that piece of shit scurry out from whatever rock he's hiding under. But the war between wanting to please her and needing to be in her presence is heavy and bloody. I'm fighting against myself, against time, against the fucking world.

Her head rests on my shoulder and a blanket drapes over us. The fuzzy kind that she loves. Her lashes flutter and I wonder if I'm in her dreams. She's always in mine. Her lips part slightly as her breath quickens.

*She's dreaming about me.*

I graze her cheek with the back of my hand before slipping out from our cocoon to have a better angle of her. I trace her knee with my finger, slowly rising over the inside of her thigh. Her skin pebbles beneath my touch. Making my way under the hem of her dress, I'm surprised my little sparrow is bare underneath. I grin to myself. The little minx.

As if she could read my mind, a smile forms on her face and her eyes slowly rise to meet my gaze. Her eyes are heavy from sleep, but they tell me everything I need to know.

Her hand reaches, fisting my shirt and pulling me closer. A gentle kiss to her perfect lips quickly turns desperate as her fingertips find my scalp. She pulls me impossibly close, and I can feel the moment her body relaxes as my fingers find their way inside her. I swallow her moans as I tease her clit with my thumb, encouraging her closer to the ledge, but refusing to allow her to come so soon.

When I remove my hand, she sighs in frustration, causing me to smile against her mouth.

"So eager, little sparrow," I taunt her. "Be a good girl and beg for it."

"P-please," she obeys as her legs fall open and her hips thrust forward slightly, begging for friction.

"You can do better than that," I tease.

I could take her right now, but Declan has a habit of taking walks in the middle of the night to 'clear his head' and the last thing I think he wants to see is his baby sister getting fucked on the couch.

Scooping her into my arms, I make my way to the stairs. She looks at me longingly.

Yes, I fully intend to give my little sparrow every single thing she wants tonight, but I'll make her beg.

Laying her gently on the edge of the bed, I stand at my full length to pull my shirt over my shoulders and let it fall to the floor. Her gaze is restrained, but I know she is using all of her effort to control the urge to reach for me.

"Such a pretty, patient girl for me," her eyes flutter shut with my praise. "Now be a good girl and *beg* for me."

I can't help but grin as her eyes open into defiant slits, shooting daggers my way.

"I did beg," she deadpans and my demeanor falters slightly, curious as to whether or not I've lost the moment with her. My strong willed woman does not take kindly to being controlled, though I generally have a better handle on reading her.

Leaning down to rest my arm next to her head, I feel her breath on my cheek as I lean in close to whisper, "You'll beg for this cock, my sweet sparrow."

A failed attempt to hide her moan makes my cock twitch against her slick center. I can feel her trembling beneath me as I draw back slowly to look down at her. The static between us thickens until it has completely consumed my every thought.

"Say it, baby." I coo, slowly torturing us both. Grinding myself against her, I strum the apple of her cheek with my thumb.

Her lips press together as she juts her chin away, refusing to conceded. *Brat.*

"That's how you want to play this?" I ask as a final warning.

My words are met with a heated gaze and I give her no time to change her mind. Shifting my hand to grab a hand full of her hair at the nape of her neck, I bring the other plam to cover her lucious, defiant lips while I line myself up at her entrance. Her breath is labored, but her body falls relaxed beneath me.

"If your mouth won't beg, your body will," I taunt. Her nails slither down the skin of my back until she latches onto my hips, encouraging me. It's all the permission I need.

With one thrust, I seat myself inside her as I capture her moan with my palm. Her eyes roll, fluttering shut but that won't do.

"Eyes on me, sparrow," I demand, as I withdraw in a painfully slow fashion, leaving us both wanting more.

With each lazy yet intentional thrust, she mewls, aching for release. My skin heats as we exchange breath, our lips but whispers against each other. Her hips rise in an attempt to keep me close, but her body is weaker than her mind and I can feel the frustration she battles to keep at bay.

Releasing her mouth and hair, in one fluid motion, I slide an arm around her waist to cradle her impossibly close. Her hands graze the skin of my shoulders before connecting behind my neck.

"I'm fading away," she speaks just above a whisper. Tears gather, threatening to fall as I hold her like the cherished and precious treasure that she is.

"Take me with you," I beg, yearning to follow her into every universe, every world, every eternity.

The air around us thickens, blocking out the reality of the pending tragedy that looms in the dark corners waiting to strike. Her eyes plead with mine. I would trade places with her in an instant, but death would still separate us. Fate is truly cruel, but how fortunate I am to have shared the breath that currently leaves her lips and dances across mine. The taste of her lingers in every atom of my being.

"There isn't a corner of the universe I could hide in, Ryde. You'll come for me. I know you will."

Tracing the outline of her jaw with my thumb, I savor the feeling of her flesh against mine. So close, but not for long. "Always, sparrow. I will always come for you."

# Chapter 49

## *Devina*

"**Y**ou can't tell him." I sip my coffee as Taylor sits across from me, marinating in the new plan I've formulated. He hates it.

But it doesn't matter. No one says 'no' to the dying girl.

"Vi, we can take care of this now. Right fucking *now*." He sits back in the chair, kicking his leg over the other, resting his ankle on his opposite knee. "Ryder would fucking do it himself. He told you that."

"That's because he doesn't know who the target is," I return, eyes shifting around the restaurant. Ryder reluctantly agreed to let me go when Taylor offered to accompany me.

"Maybe you should fucking tell him. Jesus, Vi. We've waited all of this time. You'll be gone soon..." His voice cracks causing my eyes to instantly water. "I can't do it without you."

"I don't want you to do it without me." I take another sip of coffee before placing it on the table. Reaching into my purse, I pull out three letters. "When the time comes, it'll be Ryder's decision. I've made peace with it. This is my choice," I say sternly. He knows I've had so few and I doubt he'll deny me this.

I place the letters on the table and slide them across to Taylor. He looks at the pink envelopes with sadness and rage. He'll hate me for a while, but he'll love me after. He always will.

"And what do *I* get to choose?" he huffs, looking away. I know his world was forever changed that night. I know he wants Cap dead. But he was never the one who was going to kill him. And because of that, I carry no guilt for not giving him the option now.

"He'll make the right choice. And when he does, you get to choose to live." I smile through my tears as he angrily bats his away.

"Fuck, Devina. This is not how it was all supposed to go." He sighs as he picks the envelopes from the table before scanning through them.

*MaryClaire. Declan. Taylor.*

I hold a fourth letter in my hand, but I know that I'll give it personally.

Before we leave the café, he pulls me in tight as he rests his chin on top of my head.

"God, what am I ever going to do without you?" His chest rattles with sobs.

I look up at him, wiggling my arms up to cup his face in my hands. "Live for both of us."

# Chapter 50

*Devina*

⊣||⊪|⊪ Doomsday — Lizzy McAlpine ⊪||⊪|⊢

F our weeks have come and gone. Four weeks since I faced death. Again. And in the moment when I could have given in, I fought. I fought to stay here. I fought because of the people around me. I fought to stay with him. I fought because the thought of another person deciding when I die was devastating enough to make me crazy.

But every day my body grows weaker. The bags under my eyes, darker. The nausea is the worst part. I'm so hungry.

Four days ago, I had my first seizure.

My vision hasn't been the same since.

I'm slowly fading.

*Withering.*

I know I can no longer be the one to complete my mission. Not because my body has betrayed me, but because when you lose someone you love, they take a piece of you with them. I can't do that to Ryder. Killing his father would be killing a piece of him.

I haven't failed. I won. I have Ryder, which is more than I could have ever hoped for. I was able to give him all of me. Every jagged, scratched, dented, broken piece of me. And he took it all. He begged for it.

So, I chose this.

I *choose* this.

One day, very soon, there will be no more choices to make.

The sun is beaming in through the sheer curtains in our room. I can feel it before I open my eyes to see it. Ryder sits at my side, brushing my hair out of my face. "So fucking pretty. *My* pretty girl," he whispers.

I can only smile. My mind is thinking of the words. All of the words I want to say, but my mouth doesn't always cooperate these days. It's like the thought is being translated by telephone, the game you played in grade school. By the time the information gets to the last person, it's only a skewed version of what it was originally supposed to be. But he doesn't need to hear my words. He can feel them. He can feel *me*.

I feel weak.

I feel burdensome.

I feel like I'm ready. Ready to go.

I don't hate myself anymore. Ryder's love transformed me and for the first time, I truly don't want to die. In another life, we would have had more time to be happy. We would have had children and we would have spent our days doing adventurous and mundane things. He would take me to Italy. We would have a nighttime routine for the kids. There would be first steps and first words. When we welcomed the coming years we would celebrate the last time we played pretend and the last first day of school. We would take vacations and make memories. When we were old we would look back at what had been with smiles and appreciation. But today, I can only look toward a future that would never be with longing.

As the thoughts float around me and I mourn a life that would never be, I can't help but be comforted by the idea that whether we had fifty years or only five minutes...there would never be enough time to love Ryder. But a love like ours stretches beyond time itself.

I imagine death approaching, reaching her hand out to me. There was a time when I would have gone willingly without regret. I yearned to be taken to the other side. But to be in a world where I cannot feel his fingertips caress me or hear his voice whisper my name feels hellish.

I drift back to sleep, feeling the warmth of his body against mine. I want him to always remember me as his pretty girl.

# Chapter 51

*Ryder*

〜〜 The Other Side — Ruelle 〜〜

I lay at her side as she drifts back to the sleep that calls her more frequently. I'd give anything to freeze this moment. This time with her. Every second, a memory treasured, and every breath, a loss to a demon I could never conquer.

My hand rests at the base of her throat. Just as she likes. Her pulse is steady and strong. *She* is so strong.

I fight for a memory created before her. Nothing comes. No birthday parties. No graduations. Nothing. Because my life didn't start until I began to exist in her world.

I vowed to love her until death.

That was a fucking lie.

When death forces us apart, I will love her eternally. I'll love her in this life and the next. I'll seek her out in every corner of the universe. My soul will be drawn to hers until I capture it again.

She stirs, turning toward me as her eyes flutter open.

"You're a creep, you know that?" She smiles through a heavy gaze, stretching her arms above her head. She's back to herself today.

"But you still love me," I tease. She's never spoken the words. I know she does, but she thinks saying them will break my heart. I know that hearing them now will just be another version of goodbye.

Her hands drop down, grazing the side of my face. I catch her wrist, cupping her palm to my cheek. I'm addicted to her touch. I'm a fiend for her skin upon mine. I fucking crave it.

Her eyes spark as I kiss her palm and lower her hand to wrap around my achingly hard cock. I've been waiting for hours. The silent torture of having her body heat radiate between us and not touching her as she rests makes a heavy growl fester in my chest as her fingers tenderly grasp me.

I pull her by her waist to straddle me. She runs her hands up my chest as she works her already wet cunt against me. My head pushes back against the pillow as I hold her hips firm to me wanting to savor this delicious moment.

I lift myself just enough to stroke up her back, bringing her back down with me. Her front flush with mine, I capture her face, holding it centimeters from mine. My eyes bore into hers and a jolt of electricity sends shivers down my spine.

She lifts up enough only to lower herself onto my weeping cock. Her breath syncs with mine and she makes love to me like it's our last time. As a tear escapes, slowly making its way down her cheek, I know she believes that to be just as true.

I bring her face to mine, tasting her tears. The salty liquid unlocked the core memories of her lips around my cock, taking me deep until her makeup smeared down her cheeks.

I roll her onto her back, gazing down at the masterpiece that is my little fucking sparrow. I memorized the hue of green in the eyes that captured my soul. Pulling her arms up, trapping her wrists with one hand, I use the other to trace the spackle of scars that dance on her arm. The same that now resides on my own. The piece of her I wish I could fix. Not for my sake, but for hers. I fist the hair at the nape of her neck as she eagerly tilts her head giving me better access to bite and suck.

Pumping in and out of her slowly, her back begins to arch and I know she's close. Our breaths are labored, but we don't say a word.

There's nothing either of us can say and we refuse to say goodbye. But this is what it feels like.

*Goodbye.*

I release her and she lets my hands roam, capturing the precious feeling of being in her. On her. With her.

Her hands find my hair, as they always do.

I kiss her chest, licking and biting my way down. As my teeth clamp around her nipple she hisses, gripping my hair tighter, but I won't stop. It only makes me want to devour her more.

"First, you're going to come on my hand, sparrow." I pull out of her only to replace my cock with three fingers, working her clit with my thumb.

She tenses around me, moaning as she reaches her peak. I give her a moment to recover, but only a moment.

"Then you are going to come on my tongue." She whimpers in response as I dive in, starved for my favorite meal, which may very well be my last.

My fingers remain in her, pumping her toward the next climax. Her cum runs down my hand and wrist, pooling on the sheet below us. Her legs begin to quiver when I flatten my tongue, applying the pressure she desires most and she cries out as she soaks my face.

Her body grows limp as I nip at the inside of her thigh, mending it with a kiss. Making my way back up to her, I trace her lips with *her*.

I kiss her deeply, her tongue toying with mine.

"What do you taste like, sparrow?" I ask.

"Yours," she breathlessly says as I enter her again.

"Mine," I confirm as I pump in and out of her, unable to control myself. "Now you're going to come on my fucking cock, Devina." Her eyes snap open to mine at the sound of her name leaving my mouth.

I'm losing her. She knows I know.

Her chest begins to rise and fall rapidly as her tears begin to fall. Her arms wrap around my shoulders, her hands digging in as if anchoring to me will help her stay. I need her to stay. I need her here with me but she's drifting.

We cling to each other. Is this the end?

My skin is on fire as her nails dig in. Her ankles wrap around my waist, securing her to me and I lift her to sit on my lap.

In each other's embrace, we hold on for dear life and jump together.

I let my breath steady as she pressed her forehead to mine.

We sit in silence. Only the sound of our labored breath surrounds us.

I hold her and she cries.

I hold her and I cry.

# Chapter 52

*Devina*

I don't remember my eyes closing, but I wake to the warmth of our room as red and orange embrace me through the curtains. I can feel his breath on my shoulder and I turn my head to face him.

This moment is one of euphoric perfection. My soul is healed. My body is painless, but I know that will only be temporary. As will everything else. I know that no moment in time will ever surpass the bliss that is feeling this man next to me, with our hearts sharing a tempo.

Memories of last night play back in my mind as I reach over to gently trace his strong jaw with my finger. He stirs and I think he might wake as a smile spreads across his face. I retract, not ready to see his eyes open. Nothing could replicate the intimacy that had been shared just hours ago. I wasn't ready to let it go. I wanted that to be how I remembered him when my time came.

There is beauty in the sorrow we shared. A sorrow so engulfing that my heart twitches as I recall the depth. We picked up the breadcrumbs left by evil men and used the broken pieces of ourselves to make the other whole, fitting together as the most beautiful mosaic.

I still can't bear the thought of looking at his face when he'll realize who the evil man who created such pain and wreckage was. But, the time will come soon and when it does, I won't have to be here to answer any questions.

He reaches out without waking to take me in his arms and my breathing stills. I want to stay here, *right here*, forever. But I've already decided. This is where it has to end.

I close my eyes, memorizing the moment. His hand naturally slides up my chest to rest at the base of my neck and like every day before, I feel safe and treasured.

"I love you, Ryder," I whisper, my lips grazing his softly. I feel his mouth part into a smile. The words aren't nearly as difficult to say as I thought they would be. I wish I could shout them out to the world. But this is just for him. For us.

Reluctantly, I open my eyes with a new purpose—a new freedom in mind. I slowly slip away from him, knowing that our hearts will find each other again. Knowing that no world exists, where they won't.

# Chapter 53

*Ryder*

*I* love you, Ryder.

The sound of her voice echoes in my hazy mind. I replay it again and again as I come to. It's the most beautiful sound I've ever heard. I wake to an empty bed. A pink envelope that looks all too familiar rests on her pillow where I could have sworn she was just lying. My hands shake as I reach for it, dreading its contents.

*My dearest Ryder,*

*I spent too much of my time believing that the hunt would bring me closer to her, closer to peace. But instead, it brought me to you. I will always mourn her...but you helped me to stop mourning the part of me that was taken with her. To be the recipient of your fullness, your kindness, your touch, your heart...is both all-consuming and unbearable.*

*I couldn't do it, Ryde. I couldn't take something from you, even when he took everything from me. Because the irony is that, without him, there is no you. And you, Ryder...you are everything.*

*Take the time you need to hate me, but don't grieve. We did enough of that together. Too much, I'd say. Once you're done, remember our mirrored souls and the promises we made. Then, remember that you love me and hold onto that until your own time runs out.*

*If fate is kind enough to allow us to bring some memories with us, I'll be remembering the way your lips slightly part right now as you sleep. I've memorized you memorizing every inch of me. I'll never forget being wrapped in your whiskey and oak scent as it clings to me long after you've let go. I'll remember the pain, but only because I don't want to forget a single ounce of us. Mostly, I'll try to remember that even in a perfect world, there would have never been enough time for me to love you, and I know that once that thought settles in your soul, you'll understand why I had to be the one to choose myself.*

*I was just a chapter. You still have a whole book to finish. When you're done here, and your next chapter begins, come for me. In this life and the next, I know you always will. But remember your promise and meet me where it all began.*

A photograph is tucked in the envelope. Trying to understand what I'm holding, the bottom of the page reads the final words that ignite my feet, pushing me from the bed.

*There are no truer words than the ones I will leave you with here. I love you deeply. I love you fiercely. I should have told you sooner. I love you for loving me, and I know you'll love me after you hate me for what I'm doing now.*

*I will love you always,*
*Your Devina*

My eyes travel to the nightstand where the drawer is pulled slightly, absent my gun. My feet ignite into motion before my brain fully catches up. I sprint down the hall, still unable to find my voice. The tears cloud my vision as I steady myself with the banister and fumble down the stairs in a panic.

I turn the corner to the study and swing the door open with a thud.

There she stands in her yellow dress, eyes gaunt and gun to her temple.

Our eyes connect and in that moment, the fear dissipates from her body. I see relief and I know that she's asking to be let go. Not from me, but from the pain. From the prison of her body that has become just as agonizing as the torture of her mind and heart. She's ready to be free. She's begging me to let her go. *Our last standoff.*

Time stands still. I can feel the rage, the shame, the grief leave her and she looks frail, beaten down but victorious. *Angelic.* Her soul pleads with mine. I can feel it, I can feel *her.* And mine thanks hers for the gift of this one last intimate moment, for I cannot deny her of the freedom she so desperately deserves. Her gaze begins to drift past me and I wonder if death would be so cruel as to take her just moments before she has one last opportunity to do the only thing she could choose for herself.

But she's determined and she breaks our gaze with a soft blink. I release the letter I've been clinging to and it floats gently to the ground. In a moment of selfishness, I lunge toward her.

Her eyelids meet one final time and she pulls the trigger.

I'm too late.

I catch her as she falls to the ground. Cradling her to me, I release a sound that I've never heard before.

No.

No.

No.

You can't be gone.

You can't leave me.

"No, Devina. No. No. *No!*" I shout into the empty room.

Desperately, my hands scramble to try and piece her back together as I shatter around her.

Blood. There is so much blood.

Pieces of her are scattered against the wall behind us, dripping to the floor.

Deciding I have already spent too much time in this life without her, and full of agony, I grab the gun still in her hand.

Raising our hands to my head desperate to go to her wherever she is, I don't hesitate. I plunge.

*Click.*

*Click.*

*Click.*

She knew. She knew I'd come for her and she forbade it by only allowing for a single bullet in the chamber.

"FUCK!" I scream as MaryClaire runs into the room before coming to an abrupt halt. A deafening cry echoes in the room around us. She falls into Declan's embrace as he approaches her. Confused, he turns to look at the grotesque scene. His eyes become wide as he cradles MaryClaire and braces himself weakly against the door frame. They fall to the ground, MaryClaire's shoulders shaking with sobs.

I don't care. I can't care because I can only feel the tacky wetness sending a tidal wave through my senses.

Blood.

More blood.

The crimson fluid begins to thicken, seeping through my skin to my bones until I taste a mixture of copper with the salt of my tears.

It is then that I think of her green eyes fluttering to mine as the sun shines through our sheer curtains. I remember the feeling of her soft cheek against my fingertips, as I cradle her and hold what is left of her head against me. I remember her voice as she purrs my name just before drifting off to sleep. I remember the last words she gifted me.

*I love you, Ryder.*

I remember my last promise and I know what has to be done. I gently place what is left of her on my lap, frozen in place, as people begin to move around me.

"I'll come for you, my little sparrow. I'll come for you."

A whispered promise that I will keep in this life and every one after.

# Chapter 54

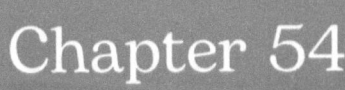 

*A moment to mourn*

⣀⣀ The Silence — Morgan Clae ⣀⣀

# Chapter 55

*Taylor*

⑴┃⑴┃⑴ Last November — MGK ⑴┃⑴┃⑴

Sun heats the room as it spills in through the colored glass of the church. Each sob echoes, creating a chorus as it ricochets against the walls around us.

We sit in the first row. MaryClaire, Declan and Ryder to my right. Fiona stands at the closed casket of my best friend, kissing her fingers before placing them gently on the rich dark wood. Her shoulders sag in defeat.

She turns slowly, yet as her feet begin to drag her away, her fingertips linger as if wanting to hold on to the very last moment she will be in Devina's presence. She doesn't take her seat next to me, but continues past me. The clacking of her shoes echo through the church as she makes her exit. Ryder gave her the option to stay on– as family. We all knew she would be leaving. She couldn't fathom being in the home that Devina passed in. Who could blame her?

I, on the other hand, could barely bring myself to leave it to come to the funeral. I need to be in a place where I feel surrounded by her, or it all becomes too real and the pain of her absence will surely drag me to the darkest depths of hell.

It's my turn, but I can't seem to make my feet move. MaryClaire reaches over Declan to place her tiny palm on my knee, effectively snapping me out of my haze.

I climb the three steps to Devina. Well, what's left of her.

I've already cried. Alone and with her. I already said my goodbyes, but no one knows that. They don't fault me now. They think I'm in shock. In a way, I still am.

When the shot rang out, followed by Ryder's screams, I sat at the edge of my bed knowing what she did. I'd known it would happen. I'd known it would happen like that. In the morning, when everyone was asleep. For seven days I sat at the edge of my bed waiting for the shot. As the days went on, I soaked in every opportunity to see her smile and watch her love the people around her. On the eighth day, it happened.

MaryClaire's shrill scream sent me into a spiral. With my devastation festering deep inside me, it was the key that unlocked my rage. With one swipe, I cleared the frames and vase from the dresser, watching glass shatter around me. Dropping to my knees, I sobbed.

I had been force-fed loss my entire life, until my body made room for the grief. Now it is just an extra weight I've adjusted to carrying around on my shoulders.

My heart broke but I know it's what she wanted. I know it's what she needed to be free.

She blushed when Ryder called her his sparrow. I saw it the morning of their wedding. I couldn't be there, but I was watching through the cameras I'd installed. I couldn't hear them, but his departure left her breathless and curious. She later confirmed what he said.

Devina was a sparrow. Born to be free and feel the wind against her face as she soared. She wasn't made to be caged and hung like a trophy. She was made to explore and be admired for the kind of beauty only nature can bestow upon you. Her voice was a song. A melody that carried straight to your soul, leaving you breathless and wanting more.

MaryClaire's sniffles bring me back to the present. I bowed my head to whisper my last words of love and promises. It's mostly for show. I really want to curse her for leaving me. I want to stay angry. But how do you stay angry at someone for dying on their own terms when death is waiting on the porch, ready to kick the door down?

MaryClaire and Ryder took their turns saying goodbye.

Ryder's shoulders slump as he kneels to place his forehead

against her casket. Tears flow freely as he holds onto the pink letter she left him. A letter similar to the ones I'll have to pass out shortly. The one I still haven't brought myself to read. His whispers dance through the space, though I cannot hear what he's saying. I know he's made his choice, though. I know what he will do next. And while I am internally bracing myself for the aftermath, I understand the amount of love he carries for her and know it's the only thing left for him to do.

Music plays as the ushers surround her to carry her to the grave site.

On top of the hill, she is lowered below. Rain begins to fall. *She's with us.* I look to the sky and let her tears kiss my cheeks. She didn't want to leave, but death would not allow her to stay. Death, I've learned, is a real son of a bitch.

Ryder stands at the foot of her grave. His posture is stoic, but I know his heart is still stained by her blood and tissue. He gives us a nod, dismissing us without words. I know he has none. I gently place my hand on the small of MaryClaire's back to guide her away. Declan follows, silently. MC didn't know Devina long, but I could see the genuine love they shared. She filled the gaping hole in Devina's heart that was made the night Scarlet was taken from her. Seeing her so frail today is a stark contrast from the usual bubbly version of MaryClaire I tolerate. As she leans into me to keep herself standing, I secretly would give anything to have the normal version of her right now.

The silence feels like static against my skin as the cars bring us back to the estate. I exit first, lending my hand to MC as she slips her dainty feel on the gravel. We stand in a circle for a moment, knowing that once we depart, life will somehow have to move forward. Removing the envelopes from my jacket, I feel the weight of them in my palms. The last pieces of her that I must hand over to the people she loved most. There is understanding in their eyes as they accept the only closure they've been bestowed.

Anger festers in my chest as they look at me with gratitude for handing them the final words of our dear friend. If only they knew... I knew this would happen. I *let* this happen. If they knew, they'd hate me.

Staring at the pink envelope on my dresser, I curse Devina for leaving how she did. She was my best friend, my little sister. I knew her better than she knew herself, which is why I knew that talking her out of her plan was impossible. Once she's made up her mind about something, you're either going to help her or get the hell out of the way.

Needing something to numb me, and having given Devina the rest of my stash, I decide on something more...legal.

I head down to the library to break open one of Ryder's whiskeys, only to find him already there, sitting in one of his oversized leather chairs.

"What's the cure tonight?" I ask approaching.

"Scotch." He doesn't look at me. His eyes are trained on a piece of paper.

I pour my drink and make my way back toward him, seating myself across the small table from him.

He takes one last swig, emptying the contents of his glass before tossing the piece of paper on the table. It's a photograph. I don't reach for it. I know what it is.

"Did you know?" he asks, his eyes finally meeting mine.

"Yes." There's no point in lying. He can throw me out. Devina isn't here anymore.

He wipes his face with the palm of his hand. I brace myself. I know how to gauge Ryder in Devina's presence. Without her, he could certainly fly off the hinges. Fuck, I'd put a bullet in my head if I were him.

*Too soon?*

Not that it would bring her back, but it might make me feel better for a minute or two.

"It was him." A statement, not a question.

"Yes," I confirm, staring at the picture of his father.

My breathing stalls. I know I can't sway him. He's already made his decision. I saw it happen earlier, but the energy palpitating in the room right now confirms my suspicions. He has to make this decision on his own. Nico's death was planned justice for my mother as much as it is for Scarlet, but I'm not sure he knows that part of the story or cares. I'd give anything to have my best friend back, to have my mother back. But I'd settle on watching the life leave that motherfucker's eyes.

He stands, placing his glass on the coaster.

"I know what you need me to do, sparrow," he says to her, ignoring me.

Devina came to him broken, a shell of herself. He loved her back to who she was meant to be.

To know that kind of love is as rare as it is to catch a sparrow.

# Chapter 56

*Ryder*

⑈|⑈ Skin and Bones – David Kushner ⑈|⑈

*C*hest to chest in the library, she stands blindfolded before me. Her cinnamon hair is pulled back into a loose braid that hangs down her back.

"Can I open my eyes now?" she asks, trying to hide her smile. I know she loves surprises, but she won't like this once I give back her vision.

"I need you to take a deep breath. When I take this off, I want your eyes on me, sparrow." I command.

She bites her lower lip in anticipation and I plant a kiss on her forehead before removing the fabric from her face. Her expression quickly drops as she takes in the room around us.

Candles illuminate the space around us. So many, you would think it was daylight. Terror strikes her gaze and I feel her shoulders become stiff under my grip.

"Why would you do this?" she asks with a whisper, tears pooling in the corner of her eyes.

"Eyes on me." She obeys immediately while letting a single tear escape.

I can feel the terror radiate from her skin, boiling right below the surface. There's a chance she'd take off and run, but that would mean passing through the candles that surround us closely. Only a single path is available, but it's behind her and she's too scared to move.

I want her to conquer her fear. I want to remove the terrible memories that plague her. I want to replace every fucking memory she had before me.

*I begin to slowly circle her as she trembles.*

*"I want to remind you, sparrow, that if I had to burn the world for you, you might have to get close to the flames." She whimpers as I caress her arm with the back of my fingers. "This is the dark world we live in. But once the world has been engulfed in the fire, I will extinguish every flame until there's nothing but embers. You'll never be burned again."*

*I turn her around to face me and begin to walk across the room toward my large oak desk. Her hand reaches out to me, but I'm just out of reach.*

*"Ryde, please," she quietly begs. "Please put these out."*

*"I need you to walk to me, Devina," I gently urge, leaning back against the desk. My arms fold over my chest.*

*She slowly lowers herself to her knees and begins to sob. She's so much stronger than this, but I know the memories are replaying in her mind. She needs to focus on me. I need her to know I'll always protect her.*

*"I can't," she pleads with her head bowed.*

*"Then you'll crawl to me." The words make her eyes snap to mine. She may be terrified, but I know she's clenching her thighs together, wanting me to give her a release. We silently hold our gaze as tension builds. This is what we do. But I won't break first.*

*Slowly, she inches toward me, her black dress cut perfectly above her knees. I hold her gaze with intensity. She lifts her chin. She'll always obey, even when she isn't happy about it. I was ready for her before we stepped into the room, but now I'm aching to be inside her, to reward her bravery. As she inches closer, I kneel to her level, catching her quivering chin in my palm.*

*"Look how well you did for me, sparrow." I know she'll gush for the praise. "Are you ready for your reward?"*

*Her breath hitches as I readjust my hand to the column of her throat, lifting her from the ground to her feet. A blanket of desire covers the fear until it's snuffed. She hasn't noticed that many of the candles have burned themselves out and the light around us has simmered to a soft glow.*

*"Yes," she says, breathlessly.*

*Keeping my hand snug against her throat, I use the other to wrap around her waist, lifting her in the air. Her legs work quickly to wrap around me and she connects her ankles, bringing her impossibly close.*

*Turning to face the desk, I gently lay her over the cold wood. Leaning down, close enough to feel her breath on my lips, I continue my praise. A simple 'good girl' would not suffice.*

*"You're so brave, my sweet sparrow." I let my lips touch hers, but don't permit a kiss. Her tiny fingers grasp my crisp shirt to pull me closer. "You're so fucking strong." I drag my lips across her skin and down her neck. She arches her back to give me access to her sensitive skin. "You're a masterpiece," I proclaim as I reach around to pull her scarred arm away from me to pin above her head.*

*"Are you ready for me sparrow?" I taunt. Her whimper is all the confirmation I need.*

The memory plays back as I enter a room with dark navy walls. Bookshelves line both sides of me and I trace my finger along the spines as I make my way toward the chair near the window. The only light guiding me is from the streetlight outside. I take a seat and pull a cigarette from my suit pocket. I inhale and think of her. It's been ages since I've stepped foot in my father's study, but the memory of us in the library was my inspiration.

She wouldn't believe me, but she wasn't just a chapter. She was the whole damn book. A book that hadn't begun until our eyes locked and that would never finish.

It's been two weeks. Two agonizing weeks since my sparrow has taken flight toward her next chapter. But she's left one thing unwritten, in an act of true selflessness. She could never take from me what he took from her. And while I know her innocent heart believed she was only ever meant to be a glimmer for me, I know that to be untrue. She was never a glimmer, a moment, a glimpse. She was the spotlight. She was time when time stood still. She was the vision.

I inhale.

The brass handle of the door turns and light bleeds into the room as he enters. He shuts the door and switches the light on before shaking his coat off. Fucking bastard hasn't even noticed me. He turns to face me and his face pales with shock.

"Ryde, what the hell are you doing here?" He glances down at the gun.

He knows what I'm here for.

*This is for Scarlet and Devina,* I think cocking one bullet into the chamber, but I know he's picturing the faces of everyone he has ever wronged, still trying to decide which one I'm acting on behalf of.

He's plastered to the back of the door. The man I spent years fearing, the man determined to make me as cold as he is. The man who only cared for power and would kill to keep it.

"This is for Scarlet," I say, lifting to take aim as the look of recognition paints his face at the sound of her name. I don't wait for a response. There's none that he could give that would change my mind.

As his eyes widen, I don't hesitate any longer to pull the trigger.

He falls with a thud.

It's not the grand finale that I know she would have wanted. There's no flames. But the bullet coming from my gun is the ultimate revenge.

I stand to drop my cigarette and step on it with my black loafers. Walking toward him, I notice how weak he looks. Shock is still apparent in his features.

I cock my gun once more.

My finger presses against the cold metal and heat rises to my ears.

"And this is for Devina."

The echo of the shot rings in my head and I know all that's left to do is eagerly wait for the moment she'll be mine again.

# Chapter 57

*Headline*

INFAMOUS BOSTON CAPO, NICO TOTARO, AND HIS SON WERE FOUND DEAD IN AN APPARENT MURDER SUICIDE.

# Epilogue

*Ryder*

⊪⊪|⊪ The Night We Met — Lord Huron ⊪⊪|⊪

The darkness begins to fade and I feel a shiver through my bones as I regain my vision.

They hustle around me. I can't see their faces. My eyes are fixed on the door before me. I've seen this door before but I can't remember where. I can't remember anything before now. I take several steps closer, before reaching out to touch it. It's real.

I can feel her. It all begins to rush back to me. My soul begins to simmer inside my skin. Fear is outweighed by an overwhelming need to satisfy the sound her heart makes as it beckons out to mine.

I reach for the handle and slowly turn it, fearful that I'll be met with emptiness on the other side.

I stand, feet planted in the doorway, as the door slowly swings open.

Her bridal suite is softly lit from the red and orange sky outside the window. She sits at her vanity combing her hair when our eyes connect in the reflection in front of her.

She smiles and slowly turns looking coyly at me.

"You came for me."

***The End.***

# Afterword

Dear Readers,

Thank you for reading To Catch a Sparrow. This book was written by someone with a broken heart.

If you struggle with thoughts of suicide, I will leave you with this:

They won't get over it. They won't move on. They need you here.

We need you here.

SUICIDE AND LIFELINE HOTLINE: 988

Substance Abuse and Mental Health Services Administration Hotline:

1-800-662-HELP (4357)

Be sure to read Taylor and MC's story, *Mourning Dove*, for a happy ever after that will be a balm to your soul.

# Acknowledgements

*It is said that a flock of sparrows signifies community, joy and resilience.*

As many of you know, this book was initially released in the summer of 2024, but was "unpublished" for personal reasons. Because this book was written as my personal navigation through grief, I was devastated. But you all stayed. I received numerous emails when my account went dark and felt so celebrated when I returned. Every comment and message has made me feel like we are building such a beautiful community. Every time I meet a reader, I'm elated to know my words made a difference. I will forever be grateful for your endless support and encouragement. Please know that I read every comment and message and do my best to respond. I wouldn't be here without you.

To Sabrina, my twin, my first baby and my longest love... thank you for your profound contribution to my life. Thank you for endless voice notes and for always having the perfect song. Your soul sings to mine and I wouldn't know what to do without you. I love you sissyface.

Deb, the friendship we share is what internet dreams are made of! I am so happy that we have been able to walk our own writing journeys alongside each other. I'm so proud of you friend. You are such a talented storyteller and I am honored to read whatever you send my way. Cheers!

REESEY! As I write this, you are sitting cluelessly next to me... waiting for class to start... I'm so grateful that our mental breakdowns aligned and we ended up at cosmo school together! I'm even more grateful for a friendship built on trust, kindness, understanding and overall willingness to have each other's backs through it all. You are my ride or die, girl. You may not be a reader (and will probably never read this) but you encouraged me to find my best self, and I wouldn't have made it through the hard times without you. I love you so much. You are a beautiful human and I'm blessed to know you.

There are a million people I could call out, but there simply aren't enough pages to tell you how humbled I am that you all are here, reading my stories, following along with my crazy and chaotic side quest of a life. Thank you for being such a crucial and intricate part of it all. I am eternally grateful for my flock of sparrows.

Xoxo,
EHW